A SUMMER OF LOVE

SEASONS OF LOVE SERIES
BOOK THREE

BRENDA DUKE-BARBER

Library of Congress Catalog Card Number: 97-94424

ISBN 1-57502-603-1

Printed in the USA by

MORRIS PUBLISHING

3212 East Highway 30 • Kearney, NE 68847 • 1-800-650-7888

To the greatest Pastor & his Wife,
Rev. & Mrs. Tim Copeland.
Thanks for taking me and my family under your wings and being not only a pastor but a friend.
You are the best!

Table of Contents

Chapter One

The New Teacher

The summer was swiftly passing, and Joy Louisa hoped the school board would find her a teaching position; however, now, she hoped for the opposite. If she could by some means teach in Hollow Creek that would be fine; but, she knew that would be impossible. Joy Louisa felt sure Miss Lindsey, the teacher from Hollow Creek, would never leave her position because she had been teaching at the school for a long time. Joy Louisa did not want to leave; nevertheless, she thought it would be unfair to her mama and Papa John to waste the education she obtained from the school in the city.

One day John brought in the mail and there were several letters addressed to Joy Louisa. He placed them on the table because he knew that she would find them when she came down to help Ellen with supper.

When Joy Louisa finished gathering eggs for the pie that she would be preparing for their evening meal, she walked into the kitchen and found the letters that John had placed on the table. She put the eggs in the sink and picked up her letters. She had one from Camilla, and one from Hazel, both of whom she had met when she was going to school in the city. The third letter looked very business like. She glanced at the return address and found "The County School Board" typed in bold print. She raced to her room, sat on the bed and opened the envelope. She hurriedly unfolded the letter and began to read.

Dear Miss Davis,

The School Board has looked over your application for a teaching position and we find it to be very impressive. We are pleased to inform you that we accept your application. There will be two positions available for your choosing this fall. One position is in the town of Bayview.

"Bayview," Joy Louisa said aloud. "That's a long way from here." Then she continued to read the letter.

The other position is in Hollow Creek. The present teacher has sickness in her family and must return east.

"How sad," Joy Louisa said to herself. It did not register to her that this teacher was Miss Lindsey. She continued to read.

You will have first choice, Miss Davis. Please inform us of your decision as soon as possible.

The County School Board

Joy Louisa sat there a minute thinking of the positions that she was being offered.

"Let's see," she said aloud, "one position was in Bayview and the other one was..."

She re-read the letter... Hollow Creek!! She jumped off her bed and ran down the stairs to find Ellen.

"Mama, Mama," Joy Louisa called out as she ran through the house.

"Joy Louisa, what in the world is wrong with ya?" Ellen asked.

"Oh Mama, I am so excited. Look what came in the mail today."

Ellen began to read the letter. "Oh, sweetheart," Ellen exclaimed hugging her daughter. "Our prayers have been answered. Ya can stay here at home and teach our own children here in Hollow Creek."

"I am so happy, Mama. I'm sorry that Miss Lindsey has sickness in her family; but, I am glad that I can teach the children here in Hollow Creek."

When the family gathered around the table for their meal, and after Papa John asked the Lord to bless the food, Joy Louisa made her announcement.

"I would like to tell everyone that today I received a letter in the mail asking me to take the teacher's position here in Hollow Creek."

"Oh, Joy Louisa," Amy Jane exclaimed. "Thet is jest wonderful!"

"Does thet mean ya will be our real teacher," Deanna Ruth asked. She would be starting the third level this year.

"Yes, Deanna Ruth, I will be your real teacher."

"Mine, too?" Jonathan Mark asked.

"Yes, Jonathan Mark, yours, too," Joy Louisa answered.

"Will you be my teacher when I go to school too?" Ernest asked.

"Yes, Ernest Paul , yours too"

"Oh goody, goody, Joy Lou Lou is my teacher."

Ernest Paul was the only person who called their sister, Joy Lou Lou. Joy Louisa did not mind. Ernest Paul had been very sick as a baby and the doctor told them that he would not live. Joy Louisa remembered how she prayed for hours that Ernest Paul would live. After he came through all the complications, Joy Louisa would have let Ernest Paul call her anything.

After supper, Joy Louisa wrote a letter to the school board accepting the position for the Hollow Creek school.

****

She anxiously waited for the official reply. Finally, it arrived, stating that Mr. Hargrove would meet her at the school on Monday. Joy Louisa was so excited she could hardly sleep the night before she was to meet with Mr. Hargrove.

The meeting with Mr. Hargrove went extremely well. He was pleased with her becoming the new teacher. She was so excited that her prayers had been answered. She, Joy Louisa Davis, would be a real teacher. She held in her hands the certificate that Mr. Hargrove had given her.

"Thank you, Lord!" she prayed.

She cleaned the school room before she left for home. She then walked through the teacher's living quarters. Miss Lindsey had cleaned everything before she left. The rooms were all in order.

Joy Louisa decided it would be best for her to move to the teacher's quarters at the school. She hated leaving Amy Jane again; but by living at the school, Joy Louisa could have the stove burning during the winter. She would pack her belongings once again, and ask Papa John to move her things to the school.

As she closed the door to the school house, once again, she prayed, "Thank you, Lord, for answering my prayers."

The next few days were busy ones for Joy Louisa. She packed her things to be moved to the rooms at the school. She was excited as Papa John began to load the wagon.

Amy Jane went with Joy Louisa and Papa John to the new "home" of Joy Louisa. When they had all of Joy

Louisa's things out of the wagon and into the house, Papa John returned to the fields. Amy Jane stayed to help Joy Louisa put everything in the proper places.

By the time they completed their tasks and cleaned the rooms, both girls were exhausted. They sat on the couch to rest, and that is where Ellen and John found the two sisters, asleep.

"Joy Louisa, Amy Jane," Ellen called out as she entered the school. When there was no answer, she walked into the living room. "Bless their hearts," Ellen said.

"My, they're all tuckered out, I do believe," John said.

Ellen walked over and touched Joy Louisa on the shoulder and she jumped with fright.

"I didn't mean to scare ya, sweetheart," Ellen said.

"That's all right," Joy Louisa said laughing. "We sat down to rest for a minute, and we really did rest."

"Boy, we jest rested good," Amy Jane laughed.

"Come on, ya two," John said, "y'all need a good supper and then some good rest."

"This looks very nice," Ellen said looking around the room. "Y'all did a fine job."

Joy Louisa was excited. In three days she would begin teaching at the Hollow Creek school. After supper, Amy Jane helped Joy Louisa with the dishes. As the two sisters worked together, they talked about Joy Louisa leaving home.

"Well, at least, yo're still close by," Amy Jane said as she dried the dishes.

"Yes, I'll be home probably every Saturday and I know I'll be here for Sunday dinner," Joy Louisa replied.

****

The first day of the new school term was an exciting day. The students were as happy as their new teacher. Joy Louisa had arranged the classroom with the girls on one side and the boys on the other side. She remembered her first day of school when Elmer Jackson put her pony tail in his ink well. She had always said from that day forward, if she ever taught school, she would have the boys sitting across the room from the girls. Now on her first day of teaching, that was exactly how she put the students .

After everyone settled down in their desks, Joy Louisa lead the class with the pledge of allegiance to the flag, and then with prayer. She gave the older students their reading assignments, while the younger students wrote their alphabet. After lunch she read a story to them. Before Joy Louisa and the students realized it, the school day was over. *All had gone well*, she thought to herself.

As soon as all the students left, Joy Louisa began to clean the board and straighten the room. When she completed that job, she sat down at her desk to look over the next day's assignments. She opened her desk drawer and out jumped a frog into her lap. She jumped up screaming. She knew Bozy Abbott was responsible for this act. He was the oldest of her students and he tried to take over the class. She would certainly deal with this situation tomorrow.

Finally, after getting her nerves calmed, Joy Louisa began to look over the next day's assignments. She put every thing in order, and closed the school room door behind her. Then she remembered the frog. She went back into the school room to see if she could locate it and sweep it out of the room. *All I need tomorrow is for a frog to start jumping all around the room,* she thought. She had made it through the first day of school.

Chapter Two

Amy Jane's Shocking News

A few days later Joy Louisa closed the door to the school and went to her kitchen. She sat down at the table exhausted. The big boys had given her a lot of problems. She attempted to gather her thoughts when she heard a soft knock at her door.

"Come in," Joy Louisa called.

When the door opened, there stood Amy Jane.

"Come in, Amy Jane, I need someone to talk to."

"So do I," Amy Jane replied.

Joy Louisa noticed that Amy Jane looked sad, "What's bothering you?" Joy Louisa asked her sister.

"Well, I've been a thinkin' 'bout my real mama lately. I would like to go South an' find my mama's family."

"Amy Jane," Joy Louisa gasped. "Are you serious?"

"Yes, Joy Louisa, I am very serious."

"But you don't even know your mama's people. How will you find them?" Joy Louisa asked with concern.

"Papa knows them," Amy Jane answered.

"Yeah, I guess you're right. Have you talked with Papa John and mama?"

"No."

"Amy Jane, you really need to think about this. More importantly, you need to pray about this."

"I have, Joy Louisa, for a long time," Amy Jane said with tears in her eyes.

"Amy Jane, I'm sorry. I know you will do the right thing. It's just..."

"I know," Amy Jane replied. "It's really scary, but I must go. Ya really don't understand, Joy Louisa. Ya've known yo're grandma an' grandpa fer a long time. I don't even remember mine."

"It must be sad not to have a real Maw Maw, but my Maw Maw loves you as much as she does me. And Mama, what will she do without you?" Joy Louisa asked with concern.

"I know Maw Maw loves me and I love her. And Mama..." Amy Jane fell silent with tears streaming down her face.

Joy Louisa walked over, put her arm around Amy Jane and cried with her step sister. Both girls were silent for a few minutes. Each was having thoughts of her own.

"I'll miss you, Amy Jane."

"I'll miss ya, too, Joy Louisa. Ya'll never know how much I have admired ya as we was a growin' up. I always wanted to be jest like ya. I was proud to tell everyone thet ya was my sister."

"Oh, Amy Jane. I love you so much," Joy Louisa said through sobs. "You are a great sister."

The young ladies stood embracing each other as tears streamed down their faces.

"Joy Louisa," Amy Jane began after several minutes, "please help me pray. I want to do the right thing. I want to go an' I want to stay. The main reason thet I want to go is to make sure my mama's family knows the Lord as she did."

"Did Papa John say whether or not your mama's family knew the Lord?"

"He said thet Grandma and Grandpa were Christians, but Aunt Catherine an' Uncle Leon did not go to church when Mama an' Papa left to come west."

"Where do they live?" Joy Louisa asked.

"Atlanta."

"Atlanta?!" Joy Louisa gasped. "Thet's a mighty big place. Oh, Amy Jane, the southern people have slaves."

"I know, Joy Louisa, but thet's jest a way of life."

"No, Amy Jane! It's not right, having people as slaves."

"Well, maybe my folks don't have slaves. I don't know, 'cause I don't even *know* my folks."

"I will certainly help you pray about this. When are you going to tell Mama and Papa John? They will be so sad."

"I know they will. I'm not sure jest yet when I'll tell them."

After Amy Jane left, Joy Louisa sat down at the table. She laid her head on the table and wept. She began to think of how her mama had told the story of when Amy Jane became a part of their family.

A wagon pulled into the yard of their little farmhouse on that very cold and snowy day. Amy Jane and her mama, Rachel, had been in the back of the wagon trying to stay warm.

Rachel was about to have a baby. In the midst of the snow storm John made a wrong turn. Instead of going into the city, he went further into the country. Ellen's house was the first house John saw, so he stopped to see if someone could help his wife.

Some time later, Rachel gave birth to a baby boy. He was very small and didn't live. Rachel also died. Amy Jane stayed with Ellen and Joy Louisa after Rachel died and John stayed with Homer and Della Ruth.

Before having to stop in Hollow Creek, John, Rachel and Amy Jane were a part of the wagon train headed to California. John planned to continue the trip in the spring after Rachel died. By spring, things had changed. Later, John and Ellen were married, making Joy Louisa and Amy Jane "real sisters."

Joy Louisa did not realize how long she had been sitting there, until she noticed that the room was growing dark. Since moving to the school, Joy Louisa prepared her meals, except on Sundays. She always ate Sunday meals with her family. At first, Ellen thought "her little girl" would never make it, but she had been doing it now for two weeks.

However, this was one night that Joy Louisa did not even have an appetite to eat anything. Everything she started to prepare seemed to give her a sick feeling in her stomach. Finally, she chose bread, jelly and a glass of milk.

After finishing her bread and milk, she washed the plate and glass, picked up the lamp and went to her bedroom. Thankful that the next day was Saturday, she picked up her Bible and began to read. She made this a habit for many years.

When she finished reading several chapters, she knelt beside her bed and prayed. She prayed for her mama and Papa John. Then she prayed that Amy Jane would do the right thing. She lay in her bed for a while before drifting off to sleep.

Awakened by the sun shining in her window, Joy Louisa jumped out of bed. She thought she would be late for school.

"I can't believe I slept so late," she said to herself. Then it suddenly dawned on her that it was Saturday. She sighed with relief. Then her mind went back to the day before.

Amy Jane had come over and told Joy Louisa about the trip to Atlanta. She whispered another prayer for Amy Jane. Joy Louisa prayed Amy Jane would do the right thing. It seemed like a big step for such a young girl.

When she finished breakfast, Joy Louisa cleaned her "little home". When she finished, she went to clean the classroom. She washed the board, swept the floor and straightened all the desk. When she completed the cleaning, she heated some water for a bath. She had just finished her bath and was combing her hair when there was a knock on the door.

"Come in," Joy Louisa called.

"Hey, Joy Lou Lou."

"Hey, Ernest Paul. How's my little brother?"

"I'm ok."

"What's going on over at your place?"

"Nothin' really."

"Did Mama send you over here to tell me something?" Joy Louisa asked, knowing that she always had to pull everything out of Ernest Paul.

"Mama wants ya to come tonight fer supper," Ernest Paul answered.

"She does? Are we having a family supper?"

"Don't know. Mama jest said to tell ya to come fer supper."

"Ok, little man," Joy Louisa said rustling her little brother's hair. "Tell mama that I'll be there."

After Ernest Paul left, Joy Louisa finished brushing her hair, put her dress on and decided to go on over to her mama's house. When she entered her mama's kitchen, she knew that Amy Jane had already talked with her parents. Ellen's eyes were red and swollen from crying and Papa John's shoulders seemed burdened with a heavy load. Joy Louisa didn't see Amy Jane anywhere.

"Hello, Mama. What can I help you do?"

"Iffen ya would, ya can put the icing on the cake thet's in the cupboard," Ellen said without turning around.

Joy Louisa silently began to put the icing on the cake. Ellen moved around her kitchen in a daze. Papa John wondered out to the barn. The boys ran around playing.

Deanna Ruth came in and said, "Maw Maw an' Paw Paw will be up here in a few minutes."

"Thank ya, Deanna Ruth," Ellen said. "Would ya get the plates an' put them on the table?"

"Yes ma'am."

The entire house seemed to be filled with sadness. Joy Louisa knew it would be a matter of time before Amy Jane would be heading to Atlanta. Tonight must be the "news breaking" dinner. For many years the family assembled together for dinner when there was something special to be told. They called it a "news breaking" dinner. Soon everyone would be gathered around the table for dinner.

Ellen had cried herself to sleep after Amy Jane had talked with her and John about desiring to go to Atlanta to locate her maternal mother's relatives. She loved Amy Jane as if she were her own daughter. John tried to assure Ellen that Rachel's people would take care of Amy Jane; however,

Ellen felt uneasy about Amy Jane making such a long trip alone.

Soon the family gathered around the table. Ellen was thinking of the news that would soon be told to all the family. She couldn't eat, it seemed her heart would burst. Della Ruth noticed her daughter wasn't eating well, and wondered if Ellen was sick. Ellen was brought back to the present when she heard John talking.

"Mama," John was saying, "this is some mighty good cookin'." He knew Ellen was still thinking of Amy Jane's trip.

"Thank ya," Ellen said with a smile to her husband. "Is everyone ready for some cake an' coffee?" Ellen asked as she pushed her chair from the table.

"I'll get the cake and coffee, Mama," Joy Louisa said. "Amy Jane, will you come and help me?"

"Sure," Amy Jane replied.

The two sisters went out to prepare dessert and coffee for the adults. Joy Louisa asked Amy Jane to help so they could talk. She was eager to know how her mama and Papa John felt about Amy Jane's decision.

"Ok, Amy Jane," Joy Louisa began when the two young ladies reached the kitchen. "What's happening?"

"Well, me, Mama an' Papa had a long talk last night."

"And?..."

"Well, Mama cried. She's 'fraid fer me to go thet far, alone."

"That is a long trip."

"Yeah, but when I explained why I wanted to go and after much pleading, I finally convinced them to let me go."

"When are you going?"

"Papa said we would send a letter to Grandma an' Grandpa Ellis. Iffen they send us a letter back saying I can come, then he would know it would be the right thing."

"But how will you send them a letter when you don't even know where they live?" Joy Louisa asked.

"Well, Papa said thet he would look through some of the old things thet was mama's an' see iffen he can find the place where they live."

"But they may have moved."

"No, they lived on a big plantation."

"Papa's gonna make the announcement after supper. I'll go to Atlanta in the spring. Iffen I hear from Grandma Ellis."

"Hey, ya girls in the kitchen, we're ready fer our cake," John called.

"We're a comin'," Amy Jane answered.

When the cake had been eaten and the small children had gone outside to play, John pushed his chair back.

"Well," he began. "I have some news to break. For Mama an' me," he said taking Ellen's hand, "it is sad news."

Everyone looked at Ellen. She didn't raise her head. Tears were streaming down her cheeks. She knew what John was about to tell everyone.

"Last night," John continued. "Our little girl, Amy Jane, had a long talk with us. She has asked permission to make a trip to Atlanta."

"Atlanta?!" Della Ruth asked in shock. "Why in the world would she want to go to Atlanta?"

"Well, Amy Jane has family in Atlanta. She wants to make sure thet her mama, Rachel's, family knows the Lord as Rachel did."

John paused, then continued, "Amy Jane has prayed 'bout this fer a long time. It has laid heavy on her mind to find her mama's people. We discussed this matter with her last night fer many hours. I'll send a letter to Amy Jane's grandmother. Iffen we receive a letter from them sayin' thet Amy Jane is welcome to come to Atlanta, then she will go in the spring."

A complete silence fell among the family around the table. Ellen sat weeping silently. Amy Jane walked over to Ellen. Placing her hand on Ellen's shoulder, Amy Jane leaned over and kissed Ellen's cheek.

Then standing behind Ellen, Amy Jane, with tears in her eyes, yet a smile on her face, began to speak. "I want to say to all of ya here, thank ya so much fer acceptin' me as a part of yo're family. Ya have a very special place in my heart. I don't even remember my real mama, but this lady here," Amy Jane said, patting Ellen's shoulder, "has truly been a wonderful mama."

Amy Jane paused, blew her nose, then continued. "Uncle Edward, several months ago, ya preached a sermon thet really touched my very soul. Ya mentioned iffen we saved the world an' didn't help our own family to be saved, then we have lost the dearest thing to our hearts."

"I'm not sure," Amy Jane continued, "iffen my other family really knows the Lord as they should. I feel God's callin' on my life to tell them 'bout the peace they can have in Jesus. I'll be back. I jest want to tell them Jesus loves them."

"Amy Jane," Edward began. "We'll certainly miss ya out here, but ya must do God's will. It'll be hard fer ya mama here to let ya go. Thet's a mother's love an' concern, but God will go with ya all the way to Atlanta."

"We sure will miss ya, Amy Jane," Della Ruth spoke through tears, "but ya go with my blessin's. God will go b'fore ya an' make a way fer ya to do what he's laid on yo're heart to do."

Ellen sat silently. She was sure every one would be against Amy Jane going to Atlanta. She was sitting here listening to her own mama telling this young lady to go ahead and make the long trip to Atlanta. What was wrong with *her* family?

Soon Ellen realized every one was leaving. She had been in a world of sorrow. Every one was hugging Amy Jane and wishing her the best.

Chapter Three

Ray's Plans

Amy Jane waited anxiously to hear from her family in Atlanta. The harvest had been gathered and winter was fast approaching. There still wasn't any news from Atlanta.

Inwardly, Ellen was happy, then she felt selfish. Amy Jane had a call in her life to tell Rachel's family of God's love. Ellen knew that she should not stand in the way of Amy Jane spreading the gospel.

Everyday, Amy Jane waited, longing for news from Atlanta. She prayed every night for her family in Atlanta. She could not understand the delay.

****

Soon fall changed to winter, bringing the cold wind and snow. A few days before Christmas, Joy Louisa closed the doors of the school. She was thankful she would not have the children for two weeks. The children had been excited about the snow, and it had been hard to keep them focused on their school work.

Joy Louisa somehow managed to get the Christmas program organized. She did not know how she accomplished that task. Tonight the children would perform the program before their parents. When the students were leaving the school, they were all trying to talk and ask questions at the same time. Joy Louisa tried to be patient with them; but, finally she rushed each one of them out the door to head for home.

As she began to straighten the room, moving the desk to make space for the platform that Ray Taylor had made, Joy Louisa thought of little Alice Jean and Cecil Tatum. Alice Jean and Cecil had come to school without a lunch. Both children were so small. They looked as though they had never eaten a real meal.

Joy Louisa had never met Mr. or Mrs. Tatum. When the Tatum family moved to Hollow Creek the older Tatum boy had come with Alice Jean and Cecil to school. He told Joy Louisa that their mama was sick and their papa was working and could not come with the small children.

Several times Joy Louisa talked to Alice Jean and Cecil about a desire to meet their mama. One day Joy Louisa told them she was coming to their house because she wanted to talk with their mama and papa.

"Oh, please, don't come to our house," Cecil had said and began to cry.

"Why, Cecil, don't cry," Joy Louisa said, kneeling beside the little boy. "Why don't you want me to visit your mama?"

"Cause Papa won't let nobody come an' see Mama. He told her iffen he saw anybody at our house he would beat her. He beats my mama all the time when she ain't got no supper fer him. So, please, don't go see my mama. I cry when I see Papa hit her."

Even though Joy Louisa had not visited the Tatum home, she often wondered about the family. For lunch she had given the two small children the sandwich she had prepared for herself. Neither child came to school wearing a coat since the beginning of winter.

When all of the other children had left the school earlier, Alice Jean and Cecil remained. They were standing by the door, so Joy Louisa asked them if they needed something.

"No, ma'am," Cecil answered. "We jest wanted to tell ya to have a Merry Christmas."

"Why, thank you," Joy Louisa replied, kneeling down to give each child a hug. "You two have a Merry Christmas also."

"Yes, ma'am," Alice Jean said shyly.

"Is your mama coming back with you tonight for our Christmas program?" Joy Louisa asked.

"I don't know," Cecil answered. "Papa had to make a trip to the city. Iffen he don't come back today, then mama said thet she would come."

"Good. I would love to meet your mama. Now run along, so you can be back for the program."

"Yes, ma'am."

The two Tatum children ran toward their home.

****

At seven o'clock, many of the students, along with their parents, started gathering at the school. The ladies prepared food for everyone to eat at the conclusion of the program. There were only a few minutes left before the program was to begin at seven-thirty and Joy Louisa wondered if the Tatum children were coming.

All the students gathered behind the curtain Joy Louisa had made. Each was putting on the costume he was to wear. Just as everyone was about ready, Alice Jean and

Cecil came behind the curtain. Their little faces were shining, and both had big smiles.

"Sorry, we're late," Cecil began. "We had to take a bath an' it's a long walk from our house. We tried to hurry."

"That's ok," Joy Louisa said smiling. "Did your mama come with you?"

"Yes, ma'am," both children answered together with a big smile on their faces.

"I am so happy. Now we need to get the program started."

The program went extremely well. The children who had special parts did very well. The other children all sang Christmas carols. All of the parents were pleased with their children.

When the program was over, Joy Louisa made her way to Mrs. Tatum. She was a frail little lady. She was smiling at Alice Jean and Cecil, when they ran to her. Alice Jean looked just like Mrs. Tatum.

"Hello, Mrs. Tatum," Joy Louisa said extending her hand to the frail lady.

"Hello, Miss. Davis," Mrs. Tatum said shyly.

"I am so happy you came tonight," Joy Louisa began. "You have two fine children. They are both very smart children."

"Thank ya."

"Now, all of you help yourself to the food. We have plenty, so eat all that you want." Joy Louisa said smiling. "I need to speak to some of the other parents."

Joy Louisa noticed the Tatums shyly preparing themselves a plate with food. *I bet they have never seen this much food. How sad,* Joy Louisa thought to herself. She continued to talk with several other parents. Everyone commended her on such a wonderful Christmas program.

Ray Taylor stood watching Joy Louisa greet the parents. He was thinking of how pretty she looked tonight. They had been friends as long as he could remember. When they were teenagers, he and Joy Louisa had attended church gatherings and parties together.

As they grew older, Ray began to realize just how much he loved Joy Louisa. He had never told her of his feelings. He feared it would end their wonderful friendship. He thought she cared for him; but, he did not know for sure her "real" feelings. He saw her coming toward him.

"Thanks, Ray, for helping me with the program," Joy Louisa said, her eyes shining.

"Yo're quite welcome. The children did a great job. Of course, they had the best teacher, an' the prettiest one, too."

"Oh, Ray," Joy Louisa said laughing.

"Joy Louisa," Ray said, taking her hand. "Can I have a few minutes of your time after everyone leaves?"

"Sure."

Joy Louisa made her way to Ellen. "Mama," Joy Louisa whispered. "Would you leave your left over food here?"

"Sure, do ya not have any food?" Ellen asked with concern.

"It's not for me, Mama. It's for Mrs. Tatum and her family. You see the frail lady with the little girl and boy beside her? The children came to school today without a lunch. All the food that is left, I'm going to give to them."

"Sure," Ellen answered. "I'll mention it to Mama an' Maw Taylor."

"Ok, but don't tell anyone else. If she found out, she might be offended. I don't know her that well. I only met her tonight."

Soon all the children and their parents began to leave the school house. Many of the children brought cookies or fruit cakes to Joy Louisa for Christmas. She had already told Mrs. Tatum to wait a few minutes before leaving. There was something for her and the children.

Joy Louisa asked Amy Jane to go into the bedroom and pick out a the gift from under the bed for Alice Jean, Cecil and Mrs. Tatum. Joy Louisa had made several extra gifts and had bought a few as well. Amy Jane picked out a doll for Alice Jean, a wooden truck with wheels for Cecil, and a scarf for Mrs. Tatum. After quickly wrapping the gifts, Amy Jane went to find Joy Louisa.

"I wrapped the gifts and put them on yo're bed," Amy Jane said.

"Thanks," Joy Louisa answered. "What did you pick for them?"

"The little doll with hair fer Alice Jean, the wooden truck with wheels fer Cecil, and a blue scarf fer Mrs. Tatum."

"That's fine, but there is an older boy and Mr. Tatum. What's in there that I can send them?"

"Well, ya had some socks."

"That would be good. Get a pair of socks for each of them."

When everyone left, Joy Louisa began to wrap up the extra food for Mrs. Tatum. She had been quietly waiting for everyone to leave. She also knew it was getting late and it was quite a walk to their house. Finally, everyone went home.

"Mrs. Tatum," Joy Louisa began. "There's a lot of food left. Would you like to take some home with you?"

"Well, ma'am, ya might need it. I'm sure they left it fer ya."

"Oh, no, ma'am. I will never eat all of this food. Please, take it with you."

"But, I don't have a way to carry all thet food home. Ya see, we walked here. I don't have a wagon."

"That will not be a problem. I have already asked my friend to come back with his wagon. It is much too cold for you to walk home."

"Thank ya, Miss Davis. I know we will enjoy this food fer a few days to come."

"I also have a present for you and your family," Joy Louisa said.

"I could never thank ya enough, Miss Davis," Mrs. Tatum said as she wiped the tears from her eyes.

A few minutes later, Ray arrived with the wagon. Joy Louisa and Mrs. Tatum wrapped the food. Alice Jean, Cecil and Ray carried it to the wagon. After all the food was put in the wagon, Joy Louisa gave the presents to Mrs. Tatum, Alice Jean and Cecil.

When Alice Jean opened the little doll, she squealed with delight. She ran over to Joy Louisa and gave her a big hug. Joy Louisa could not help but cry to think that just one little doll could make a child so happy. Cecil was also thrilled over his present. Mrs. Tatum said she had never seen such a beautiful scarf and would always remember Joy Louisa whenever the scarf was worn. Mrs. Tatum thanked Joy Louisa for the presents that she had given Mr. Tatum and their oldest son.

After everyone had opened their presents, they all loaded onto the wagon and settled close together with quilts wrapped around them. As they rode along in the clear, cold night, Mrs. Tatum hummed the Christmas carol, *Away In A Manger* to herself.

On the way back from Mrs. Tatum's house, Joy Louisa sat quietly. Ray wanted to tell her of his thoughts, but was afraid she would not understand. He wanted so much, one day, to make Joy Louisa Davis his bride.

"Joy Louisa," Ray said finally breaking the silence. "I have somethin' I'd like to talk with ya 'bout."

"Yes, Ray. What's on your mind?" she asked smiling.

"Ya are beautiful, Joy Louisa."

"Oh, Ray, is that what's on your mind?"

"Yes. Ya are constantly on my mind, Joy Louisa. I don't know how to say this, but, I love ya. I know we've always been jest friends, but, I would like for us to be more than jest friends."

Joy Louisa sat quietly for a few minutes. Deeply within her, Joy Louisa had wanted to hear Ray say those words for a long time. Since she was not saying anything, Ray thought he said the wrong thing.

"I'm sorry, Joy Louisa. I don't want anything to happen thet would end our friendship. Please, let's jest ferget thet I said…"

"No, Ray," Joy Louisa interrupted. "Please don't forget what you just said. If you only knew how long I have waited for you to say those words."

"Do ya really mean thet?"

"Yes, Ray. I really mean that."

"I love ya, Joy Louisa Davis."

"I love you, Ray Taylor."

"I do have something else thet I would like to talk with ya 'bout."

"What is it?"

"Soon after winter is over, I'm goin' to Atlanta."

"Atlanta!?!" Joy Louisa replied.

"Yes, dear, Atlanta."

"Why, Ray?"

"I have always wanted to be a doctor."

"Well, I have checked and around here there's not a school I can attend to become a doctor. So I saw in a magazine about the school in Atlanta. It's suppose to be the best. I'm goin' to Atlanta to that school. I really want to be a doctor. Our little town needs a doctor. Since Dr. Rutledge died, iffen someone gets sick, we have to go to the city. I want to learn all I can an' come back an' set up my office here. Me an' ya can be together. Ya a teachin' an' me a doctorin'."

"Ray, that is wonderful!" Joy Louisa exclaimed. "Did you know that Amy Jane wants to go to Atlanta?"

"No. Why does she want to go to Atlanta?"

"Her mama, Rachel's people live in Atlanta. Papa John has written them a letter. If they write back and say Amy Jane is welcome to come, then she will be leaving in the spring. Mama was afraid for her to make the trip alone. Now since you are going, it will be easier for mama to let Amy Jane go."

"Yes, I could go the same time as Amy Jane. Joy Louisa," Ray said taking both of her hands into his, "will ya wait fer me?"

"Yes, Ray. I will wait."

****

Two days before Christmas, Amy Jane received a letter from her grandmother.

My Dear Amy Jane,

It was indeed a pleasure to hear from our Rachel's little girl. Although I assume from the letter you are no longer a little girl.

I sincerely regret that it has taken me so long to answer your letter. My dear brother, Jessie, passed away and we had to make a trip to Charleston, South Carolina. We had not planned on staying as long as we did, but the weather turned really bad so we had to delay our coming home.

I was so pleased when I found the letter from you waiting for me when I returned home. Dear Amy Jane, you will be welcomed into our home with open arms. You will never know the many hours I sat wondering about you and your sweet mother and your wonderful father.

We were so deeply filled with sorrow when we learned the death of our precious Rachel. She was so dear to our hearts. Now that you are planning on coming to be with us, we feel that a part of Rachel will be here.

Let us know the day and time you will be arriving in Atlanta and we will certainly meet you at the stagecoach house. We are so excited! Your Aunt Catherine and her two daughters, Velvet and Agnes, are here at Gable Oaks with your Grandfather and me. Velvet and Agnes are about the same age as you are, so you will have friends your own age to show you around Atlanta.

We are looking forward to the day you arrive here at Gable Oaks. Until that long awaited day, I will try to wait patiently. God Bless you, and we pray for a safe trip for you.

With love,
Grandmother & Grandfather Ellis

Amy Jane was so excited she could hardly believe what she was reading. She, Amy Jane Clarke, was finally going to Atlanta to meet her mama's family.

When Ellen learned that Ray would be going to Atlanta in the spring, she felt better for Amy Jane. Ellen knew Ray would make sure Amy Jane made the trip safely to Atlanta.

Chapter Four

Amy Jane Heads South

Winter seemed to last forever. School could not open for another week after the Christmas holidays, because the bitter cold winds had blown in so much snow. Many nights Joy Louisa lay thinking about the Tatum family. She prayed that they had plenty of wood to keep them warm and enough food to eat.

The second day of the storm, Papa John came to Joy Louisa's place. "Yo're mama sent me to bring ya to the house," he said as he came inside. "We're in fer some bad weather an' yo're mama don't want ya over here by yerself."

"It is getting pretty bad out there. Let me get a few things, and then I will be ready to go."

"I'll be a warmin' a brick fer yo're feet. It's mighty cold. Be sure to put on some extra wraps an' bring 'long some of yo're quilts."

Joy Louisa hurriedly packed her things. She gathered a few extra quilts and took them to the living room. Papa John had two bricks on the stove getting hot. When everything was loaded in the wagon, he wrapped the bricks and placed them at Joy Louisa's feet.

"Ya wrap the quilts 'round ya good an' tight," Papa John said as Joy Louisa crawled into the back of the covered wagon.

"Do you have any quilts up front to cover up with?" Joy Louisa asked.

"Yes. I'll push the horses as fast as I can. It's startin' to really snow hard again. We'd better be a headin' on home."

Joy Louisa wrapped the quilts around her and put her feet on the hot bricks wrapped in a quilt. It was very cold; furthermore, the snow and the wind were blowing hard. Papa John could hardly see in front of the horses.

Back at the house, Ellen continued to look out the window. It had been at least an hour since Papa John had left to pick up Joy Louisa. The wind was howling and the snow was falling so hard that Ellen could not even see the barn.

"Oh, Lord," Ellen prayed. "Please watch over my husband an' daughter."

Ellen went back to the stove to stir the soup. A few minutes passed, still, Papa John and Joy Louisa had not arrived. Ellen went back again to look out the window. The wind and the snow was even more tempestuous than the last time she had looked out of the window.

In the back of the wagon, Joy Louisa was shivering. Even with all the quilts wrapped around her she was still very cold. Papa John was trying to push the horses on; however, the snow was coming down so hard it was not easy to even see the road.

He slowed the horses down some. At one point the wagon seemed to mar down in the deep snow. Papa John was afraid the wagon would become stuck in the snow.

Slowly, they made their way home. When they finally reached home both were so cold they could hardly walk. Ellen sent the boys out to take the team to the barn. She made some hot coffee for John and Joy Louisa.

For the next two days, the blizzard raged outside. John went out to check on Maw Maw and Paw Paw Graves.

He made sure they had plenty of wood stacked on their porch. Ellen prayed they would all have enough wood to last through the storm.

****

After several days of being closed, because of the snow and bitter cold weather, the school finally reopened. Joy Louisa was happy to see that all of her students had made it to class.

Joy Louisa noticed how cold the Tatum children looked when they arrived for class. Little Alice Jean's coat was too small for her, and would not even button. Cecil didn't even have a coat. He wore a couple of shirts. The two children were shivering in their seats, although the school room was quite warm.

"Before we start class, today," Joy Louisa began. "we're going to warm ourselves for the next few minutes. If you are still cold from your walk to school, you may come up and stand by the stove."

She was glad to see several others came. She did not want Alice Jean and Cecil to think the teacher was doing this just for them. The students who did not come to stand by the stove were reading silently from their readers. Slowly, the ones standing by the stove, began to go back to their desks. Alice Jean was the last to leave the stove and return to her desk.

Joy Louisa had wondered if the students had forgotten everything they had learned before the Christmas and snow break. She soon learned that while the children were closed up in the house during the snow storm, many of them had read some books. Every student showed much progress.

During the lunch recess, Joy Louisa let the children play games inside. Although the sun shone brightly, it was still bitterly cold. Joy Louisa noticed Alice Jean would stand by the stove at every afforded opportunity.

After the children departed for home that afternoon, Joy Louisa re-arranged the desks. She put Alice Jean's and Cecil's desks close to the stove. They would be warm as long as they were in school.

Just as she was finishing arranging the desks, Ray came inside the school room. He stood there admiring Joy Louisa. She did not hear him come in and she jumped with fright when he touched her shoulder.

"Do I look *thet* bad?" Ray asked laughing.

"No. I just did not hear you come in."

"I guess not with all the noise ya was a makin' movin' the desks. Why all the re-arranging?"

"Well, the Tatum children hardly have warm enough clothes. They were shivering from the cold this morning, so I let any of them that were cold stand beside the stove until they were warm."

"Being the concerned teacher thet ya are, ya a movin' their desks beside the stove."

"Yes, I figure as long as they are in school, they will be warm."

"Thet's one thing I like 'bout ya, Joy Louisa. Yo're always thinkin' of someone else and not yo're self."

****

Winter finally passed and the days became warmer. Joy Louisa was glad to see the weather change. She also knew that it was getting closer to the time for Amy Jane to go south; in addition, Ray would be leaving the same time as Amy Jane. Joy Louisa would surely miss both of her friends.

Amy Jane was excited about her trip to Atlanta and Ray was excited that he was going to fulfill his dreams of becoming a doctor. Joy Louisa was excited for both Amy Jane and Ray, yet she was sad for herself.

Joy Louisa decided after Amy Jane left for Atlanta and school dismissed for the summer, she would move her things back to her mama's house. She knew that Ellen would need help when the vegetables started coming in from the garden. They would have a lot of canning to do, and with the little ones out of school, Ellen would certainly need some help.

****

The day came when Papa John made the arrangements for Amy Jane's trip to Atlanta. The stagecoach ticket was purchased and the date was sat for the departure. Amy Jane was so excited. In seven days she would be on her way to Atlanta.

On Saturday evening, Ray came over to see Ellen and John. He wanted to talk with them before Joy Louisa came to her mama's house. Joy Louisa came to her mama's house every Saturday evening so Ray could call on her.

"Hello, Ray," Ellen said as she answered the knock at the door. "Come in, Joy Louisa ain't here jest yet."

"Yes, ma'am. I was a hopin' thet she wouldn't be here yet," Ray said. Then seeing the expression on Ellen's face, Ray continued. "I would like to talk with ya an' Mister John."

"Sure. John should be a comin' inside in jest a few minutes."

"Yes, ma'am. I talked with him a minute ago an' he said thet he would be with me in a minute. I told him thet I would like to talk with y'all b'fore Joy Louisa got here."

A few minutes later, John came inside. "Well, son, what can we do fer ya?" John asked sitting at the table across from Ray.

Ellen came to sit down beside John.

"Well, I would like to ask yo're permission to marry Joy Louisa," Ray said with a smile on his face.

"My, my," John said. "Mama, what do ya think 'bout thet?"

"I think it is wonderful!" Ellen said smiling. "Jest the other day, me an' Maw Taylor was a talkin' 'bout ya an' Joy Louisa. We figured this would happen sooner or later."

Ray smiled. "Yes, ma'am. When I told Maw an' Paw what I had planned fer tonight, Maw said the same thing ya jest said, Mrs. Ellen."

"Well, son," John said. "Ya have mine an' Mama's blessin's, an' our permission to ask Joy Louisa to be yo're wife."

"Thank ya, sir, an' thank ya ma'am. When I return from Atlanta we will marry."

That evening Ray and Joy Louisa sat in the swing together on the front porch. Ray was excited about going to Atlanta. He wanted to get as much training as quick as possible, and return to open his own practice.

Joy Louisa sat quietly listening to Ray tell of his plans. She had known for many years that Ray wanted to be a doctor. She also knew that he would make an excellent doctor because he was always eager to help someone else.

Ray took Joy Louisa's hand in his and said, "Joy Louisa, b'fore ya arrived here this afternoon, I had a talk with Mrs. Ellen an' Mister John."

"You did? Don't you always talk with them if you get here before I do?" Joy Louisa asked laughing.

"Yeah, but today, we had us a "real" talk," Ray answered grinning.

"Oh? Now what kind of "real" talk did you have with Mama and Papa John?"

"Well, I asked to have their permission to ask ya to marry me. Will ya marry me, Joy Louisa?"

"But Ray, you will be leaving in three days. We can't possibly have a wedding in three days."

"I know, sweetheart. We will marry as soon as I come back from Atlanta. It will only be fer a little while. I know it may seem like a long time, but it will pass by quickly."

"I will wait for you as long as I need to," Joy Louisa answered smiling. "Yes, Ray, I will marry you."

He squeezed her hand and said, "Ya have jest made me the happiest man in the world."

"You have made me the happiest woman in the world," Joy Louisa answered with a smile.

A few minutes later, Deanna Ruth came out to tell the happy couple dinner was ready. Ellen had sent word for Maw Maw and Paw Paw, Edward and Sallie Mae and the twins to come for dinner. Ellen knew Ray would ask Joy Louisa to marry him, so this would be another "news breaking" dinner.

As they started into the house, Ray asked, "Do ya want to tell everyone tonight?"

"Yes, knowing Mama, she has asked everyone to come for the "news breaking" dinner," Joy Louisa laughed. "So you can be the one to tell everyone. Just let Papa John know that you have something to say after dinner."

When everyone had finished their dinner and all were enjoying pecan pie and coffee, Ray told the exciting news. The entire family was so excited. Amy Jane said that she would definitely come back west for the wedding.

On Sunday, Edward made the announcement of the future wedding. Joy Louisa's face glowed with happiness; however, she hoped the time would quickly pass.

Edward told the congregation of Ray's other plans. He would also be going to Atlanta to study to become a doctor, 'which we surely need here.' There were many 'Amens' to that statement.

Edward also made the announcement to the church that Amy Jane was going to Atlanta to visit her relatives. He asked that everyone remember her in their prayers. She was going to do what the Lord had put on her heart, spread the gospel to her mama's people.

The next few days were busy for Ellen and Amy Jane. They were sewing new dresses and packing everything for Amy Jane's trip to Atlanta. Joy Louisa helped as much as she possibly could. Much excitement and yet sadness filled the house.

The day of departure for Amy Jane and Ray finally arrived. All of Amy Jane's family and all of Ray's family gathered at the stagecoach house to say their good byes. There were many hugs and tears among the crowd.

"Ray," Ellen said. "Please make sure nothing happens to my little girl."

"Yes, ma'am." Ray answered.

Just before the stagecoach driver called "All Aboard," Ray held Joy Louisa in his arms and kissed the top of her head.

"Sweetheart, I'll be home b'fore long. I'll study hard so I can learn fast."

"I will be waiting for you, Ray," Joy Louisa said, trying to smile, but tears were flowing down her cheeks.

Ray wiped the tears with his fingers, as the driver called out, "All Aboard!"

Joy Louisa stood waving until the stagecoach was out of sight. She could hardly see the stagecoach due to the tears that blinded her eyes..

Chapter Five

Trouble on the Trail

The driver of the stagecoach was Jim Overholt, who became a friend to Ray on the trip. The stagecoach left Hollow Creek with five passengers. Ray, Amy Jane, an elderly man, who had introduced himself as "Smoky" Seabolt, and a middle aged couple, Maybelle and Luther Rutherford. Maybelle was about as wide as she was tall, with Luther being a very small man.

Amy Jane sat on the back seat with "Smoky" Seabolt. Ray decided to ride on top with Jim Overholt. Maybelle, beside being a large woman, was a nosey woman as well. She asked Amy Jane question after question.

At one point Luther said, "Maybelle, let the young lady rest awhile. You've not quit talking since we got on this stagecoach."

"Oh, you hush up, Luther," Maybelle snapped.

Amy Jane noticed that Luther did not say anything else; but, Maybelle quit talking for a while. Amy Jane tried to rest; however, with the stagecoach bouncing so much, it was hard for her to rest.

On top of the stagecoach Ray and Jim enjoyed talking to each one another as they rode along.

"Who's thet pretty lady ya got with ya?" Jim asked. "Is she yo're woman?"

"No," Ray answered. "Jest a friend of the family."

"Jest a friend? How could ya jest be a friend to sech a pretty one as thet?"

"Well, I'm gonna marry her sister when I come back," Ray answered.

"Is yo're woman as pretty as her sister?"

"Well, now," Ray said. "I think she's prettier."

"It's a good thing this lady didn't come by herself," Jim was saying. "Cause it ain't safe fer a pretty lady to travel alone."

"I didn't realize thet," Ray answered.

"When we stop over in Calvert City fer the night, ya better act like she's yo're wife."

"Why's thet?" Ray asked.

"Cause iffen some of the men see her alone, they'll be after her," Jim answered.

"But she'll have a room alone. Will she be safe?"

"Now iffen I was ya," Jim was saying, "I'd put the room in my name."

"But I'll have two rooms. I can't stay in the room with Amy Jane."

"We'll figure out something," Jim replied.

They rode on for several hours before stopping for a break. The passengers walked around stretching their legs, while Jim watered the horses.

"Is everything all right with y'all?" Jim asked.

"Yes, sir," Amy Jane answered.

"Well, it's not all right for me," Maybelle Rutherford complained.

"What can I do fer ya, ma'am?" Jim asked.

"There is not one thing that you can do, sir," Luther Rutherford said. "She is just a complainer."

"Now you just shut your mouth, Luther Rutherford," Maybelle bellowed at her husband.

"Ok, let's get started back on our journey," Jim announced. He did not want to get Maybelle and Luther started at each other.

Maybelle stomped back toward the stagecoach, and Luther followed behind her like a little puppy; in addition Amy Jane and Smokey returned to the stagecoach. They all settled back in their seats as the stagecoach headed off again. Maybelle was puffed up, for which Amy Jane was thankful. There would be some peace and quiet inside the stagecoach now. Maybelle would not be asking so many questions.

"I'll tell ya what ya need to do 'bout the rooms in Calvert City," Jim said as they rode along.

"What's thet?" Ray asked.

"Ya need to put the room in the name of Mr. an' Mrs. Taylor..."

"But I can't do thet," Ray interrupted. "Thet would be a lying. We're not Mr. an' Mrs. Taylor."

"Well, I'm a tellin' ya," Jim stated. "Iffen ya go in there an' let thet lady tell them thet she wants a room alone, it ain't gonna be safe."

"What will I do?"

"Ya can stay in the room with me," Jim answered. "I'll jest take care of gettin' the rooms an' ya take care of Amy Jane."

"But how are we gonna do this?" Ray asked with concern.

"Well, now," Jim pondered. "Ya will need to make sure thet Amy Jane is in her room safe. Then ya can slip out an' come to my room."

"Ok," Ray answered.

****

After traveling for several more hours, they reached Calvert City just before dark. Calvert City was a rough looking place with several saloons. As the stagecoach pulled up at the stagecoach house, there were many people around. They were waiting for other coach lines to come for them. The hotel was beside the coach house and there were several men in and around the hotel playing cards and drinking.

"Ya see what I'm a talkin' 'bout?" Jim asked Ray as they entered the hotel.

The men stopped playing cards and all of them looked at Amy Jane. Some of the men remarked 'thet shor' is a pretty little lady.'

Jim walked up to the counter to acquire about available rooms. As Jim talked with the man behind the counter, Ray walked over to Amy Jane. The man with red hair and a big bushy beard started walking over to Amy Jane. When he saw Ray walk over to her, the man returned to his table.

"Ya need to be very careful," Ray whispered to Amy Jane.

"Yeah, I noticed," she answered.

"We are to pretend thet we are husband an' wife," Ray whispered.

"What?!"

Before Ray could answer, Jim walked over to Ray and Amy Jane. "Here's yo're key, Mr. an' Mrs. Taylor," he said loudly. "I'm sure thet ya will want to freshen up before supper."

"Yes, sir," Ray replied. "It has certainly been a long trip here for the lady."

"I'll help ya get yo're things an' carry them to yo're room, Mr. Taylor. I'm sure thet yo're wife is quite tired."

"Yes, sir," Ray answered.

"Come, Mrs. Taylor," Jim said. "Ya can help also."

"Yes, sir," Amy Jane said softly.

When the three walked out to the stagecoach, Amy Jane asked, "What's a goin' on? I'm not Mrs. Taylor. Didn't ya tell him thet, Ray?"

"Yes, ma'am," Jim answered, "but this is fer yo're own safety. Ray will be staying in the room with me. I've already told him thet he must go with ya an' make sure thet ya are safe. Then he will come to my room thet is next to yo're room."

"I see," Amy Jane answered. "I did notice how those men were actin'."

"Yes," Jim replied. "It's very dangerous fer young women to travel alone."

"I didn't know thet," Amy Jane said alarmed.

"Jest as long as the men think ya are Ray's wife, ya will be all right."

"Ok," Amy Jane answered.

Ray and Jim carried Amy Jane's things to her room.

"I'll come back fer ya in a hour," Ray said.

"Thet'll be fine," Amy Jane answered.

The room was small and hot. Amy Jane went over to raise the window. She hoped the breeze would cool the room. She pulled the curtains together so no one could see in the room. Although she was upstairs, Amy Jane still felt as if someone could see in her window if the curtains were opened.

She took a bath, combed her hair, and put on a clean dress. She could not believe this town. Hollow Creek didn't have so many bad people; furthermore, she wondered if Atlanta would be like this. She had just finished putting her hair in a twist when Ray knocked on the door.

"Darlin', are ya ready fer supper?" Ray asked loudly.

"Ya have to knock on yo're wife's door?" a man asked Ray. "I'd jest go on in there."

"Well, sir, I didn't get the key when I left earlier," Ray said.

"Oh, Lord, protect us," Amy Jane prayed as she walked to the door.

When she opened the door, the man was just going down the stairs.

"Oh, Ray," Amy Jane whispered. "Will I really be safe here?"

"Yeah," Ray answered. "When they all see us together at supper, they'll leave ya alone."

"I sure hope so," Amy Jane sighed.

Ray led Amy Jane over to a table across the room. As she walked through the dining room, she could hear comments from the men, who were drinking. She walked to the table with Ray acting as if she did not hear the men.

After they were seated, Amy Jane asked, "Ray, why in the world did ya make me walk through all those drunken men?"

"I wanted them to see thet ya was with me."

"Oh," Amy Jane sighed. "I'll be glad when we can leave this place."

Both Amy Jane and Ray enjoyed their meal. Amy Jane ordered roast beef and gravy with mashed potatoes and peas. Ray ordered chicken with green beans and potatoes. When they finished their meal, they ordered apple pie and coffee. They sat talking a few minutes longer.

"Did Joy Louisa tell ya 'bout our plans?" Ray asked.

"Yes." Amy Jane answered. "I'm so happy fer y'all. How long will ya be in Atlanta?"

"I'm not really sure," Ray answered. "I hope no longer than two years."

"Will ya be goin' back home any a'tall?"

"Prob'ly not. I'll be studyin' an' workin' an' won't take time off."

"Thet's the sensible thing to do, I guess," Amy Jane said.

"What'cha gonna do once ya get to Atlanta?"

"I'm not sure," Amy Jane answered. "I'll wait an' see how things are with mama's family."

They finished their pie and coffee and decided to turn in for the night. As they walked out of the dining room, Jim was standing in the lobby. He was talking with some other men.

"Well, Mr. an' Mrs. Taylor, are y'all callin' it a night an' turnin' in?" Jim asked as Ray and Amy Jane entered the lobby.

"Yes, sir, I believe we are. It's been a mighty long day fer the lady," Ray answered.

"Yes, it has, an' fer me too. I think I'll turn in fer the night, too," Jim said. "I'll walk on up with y'all, iffen ya don't mind none."

"Don't mind none a'tall," Ray answered.

As they started up the stairs, Jim whispered, "Ya go into the lady's room an' make sure all is ok. Thet way iffen somebody's a watchin', they will see ya go in the room with her. I'll leave my door unlocked an' ya can come on in."

"Ok," Ray answered.

Ray went in Amy Jane's room, checked every thing, then went to Jim's room. Amy Jane left the window opened a little, but made sure the curtains were drawn. She could hear much commotion going on down in the streets. She wondered if she would ever fall asleep.

She knelt beside her bed for her nightly prayer. She prayed for her family back home as well as, the new family she was going to meet. She prayed for a safe trip to Atlanta. A few minutes later she fell asleep.

****

The next morning, just after dawn and after breakfast, the stagecoach left Calvert City. Maybelle Rutherford had rested well and was talking non-stop. Smokey, with his eyes red and blood-shot from drinking too much the night before, tried to sleep.

After several hours of traveling, Jim stopped to eat lunch and to rest for a few minutes. Maybelle grumbled the entire time they were stopped.

"I do wish thet woman would shut her mouth fer a spell," Smokey said.

"Well, at least, I didn't get into somebody's whiskey bottle like ya did," Maybelle spat at Smokey.

"Yo're mouth wouldn't stop long enough fer nothin' to go in it," Smokey said.

"All aboard," Jim called. "It's time to travel."

The group started toward the stagecoach.

"Smokey," Jim said. "Why don't ya ride up top with me fer a while."

"Be glad too, mister, mighty glad too," Smokey said. "At least, I won't have to hear thet woman."

They started back on the trip and suddenly came to a sharp bend in the road. The stagecoach began to sway. There was a loud noise, and the stagecoach began to overturn. Amy Jane screamed and fell into total darkness.

"Help me," Maybelle yelled. "Somebody help me."

"Yo're all right, woman. Jest be quiet," Smokey yelled to Maybelle.

"Ya stay close to Amy Jane," Jim told Ray. "I'll check on Maybelle."

"Ok," Ray answered.

Jim walked over to Maybelle. Luther was kneeling beside his wife.

"Are y'all ok?" Jim asked.

"Yes, sir, I think so," Luther answered.

"I don't know," Maybelle complained. "I need to be checked by a doctor."

"Yes, ma'am," Jim answered. "But right now, I must help with the young lady. She has a knot on her head an' has been knocked out."

"Poor little girl," Luther said. "You need to get up, Maybelle, and see if you can help with the young lady."

"Yeah, I guess you are right," Maybelle said getting on her feet. "These men don't know what to do."

Jim returned to where Amy Jane was lying on the ground. Ray was kneeling beside her, praying. Jim knelt beside Amy Jane as well. She began to move and groan.

"Amy Jane," Jim whispered. "Can ya hear me?"

Amy Jane opened her eyes, but had a far away look, then closed them again.

"We've got to get her back to the coach house," Jim said with much concern.

"How are we going to get her back?" Maybelle cried. "We don't have a way to go."

"I'll unhook the horses an' carry Amy Jane back," Jim said. "The rest of ya will have to wait 'til I bring another stagecoach back."

Jim unhitched the horses and jumped on one. Carefully Ray and Luther lifted Amy Jane to Jim. She groaned but did not open her eyes.

"Are ya sure ya can carry her all the way back to the coach house like that?" Ray asked.

"Yes," Jim replied, "I've got to get help for this young lady."

"God bless you," Maybelle said.

"Please, pray fer us to arrive safely back to the Inn," Jim called as he rode off toward Calvert City.

Chapter Six

Amy Jane's Delay

Jim rode off with Amy Jane leaning against his chest. They had tied a rope around her to help her stay on the horse. Jim was afraid to let the horse go too fast, but he knew that he must get this lady to a doctor. He prayed that the doctor would be around when they reached Calvert City.

Jim grew tired, but he knew he must continue on. Although Amy Jane was a petite lady, still the extra weight against him made the trip slow. He checked several times to make sure Amy Jane was breathing.

"Lord, iffen ya never answer another prayer fer me, please answer this one," Jim prayed. "Let this lady be all right."

After what seemed like forever, Jim saw the stagecoach house come into view. He felt as if he could not make another mile. He knew the Lord had given him the strength to make it. Over and over he had told himself, "ya can make it. Ya can make it."

When he stopped the horse in front of the Inn, several men were out on the porch playing cards.

"Hey, ya men, help me," Jim called out. "This lady is badly injured."

The men hurried over to Jim, recognizing him as the stagecoach driver.

"Overholt, what happened?" one man asked.

"The stagecoach overturned a few miles up the road," Jim answered. "This little lady has a big knot on her head an' she's unconscious."

The men began to untie the rope around Amy Jane. Slowly they lowered her from the horse and carefully carried Amy Jane inside.

"Be careful with her," Jim instructed.

Jim followed the men into the Inn. Someone had sent for the doctor when they saw Jim ride up with Amy Jane. The men carried Amy Jane to one of the rooms and gingerly laid her on the bed. She didn't make a sound.

"She ain't dead, is she?" one of the men asked.

"No," Jim answered.

Dr. Midler arrived in less than five minutes. He began to check Amy Jane. She seemed all right except for the blow on her head.

"That's a bad looking knot there," Dr. Midler said. "We must keep a close watch on this young lady. Does she have any family?"

"Yes, sir," Jim answered. He did not want anyone to know Amy Jane was traveling alone for fear of her safety.

"Where is her family?" the doctor asked. "How did she get here?"

"Sir, we were involved in a stagecoach accident," Jim began. "I'm the driver. The rest of my passengers are up the road a waitin' fer another coach to get them."

"Are any of those who are waiting, injured?"

"No, sir, I don't think so," Jim replied. "There's another lady who was complainin', but when she saw this young lady was hurt, she fergot 'bout herself. I would like to have everyone checked out iffen ya don't mind, Doctor. I'll pay you."

"When will the others arrive?" Dr. Midler asked.

"I'm goin' now an' see iffen I can get another coach or wagon. I should be back here in a few hours."

"Good," the doctor replied. "I will stay here and keep an eye on this little lady until you come back with the others. Her husband will need to stay with her throughout the night."

"Yes, sir, I'm sure thet he will," Jim answered.

For the next few hours Amy Jane remained very still. The doctor stayed close by to watch for any changes in her condition. In the mean time, Jim borrowed a wagon and hurried down to pick up the others. He wanted to get there and back before darkness set in.

As soon as the stranded passengers heard the wagon in the distance, they began to gather up all of their personal belongings. Ray anxiously waited to hear a report of Amy Jane's condition . Maybelle was also concerned about Amy Jane. Smokey had whispered to Ray that "ole Maybelle's done fergot 'bout her aliments cause she's a thinkin' 'bout the young lady."

When Jim stopped the wagon, everyone was asking all at one time about Amy Jane.

"When I left," Jim began, "the doctor was checking her over. She still had not come to herself."

"What did the doctor say?" Maybelle asked.

"Well, not a whole lot," Jim answered. "I made sure thet she was taken care of, then I left. I knew thet y'all was a waitin' fer me an' I needed to get a wagon. I wanted to get here an' back b'fore dark time."

"Thet's a good idee," Smokey said.

All the men quickly put everything from the stagecoach onto the wagon. Luther helped Maybelle in and the others followed and then they returned to Calvert City.

Throughout the night, Ray, Jim, Luther and Maybelle stayed by Amy Jane's bedside. During the night, Luther would nod and begin to snore.

"Luther," Maybelle demanded, giving Luther a jab in his side. "You wake up! This sweet girl here maybe nigh to death's door and you a snoring ain't a helpin' her none."

"Maybelle, why don't ya an' Luther go get some rest," Ray said. "I'll stay with Amy Jane. Ya go too, Jim."

"No," Jim replied. "I'll stay with ya."

"We'll stay too," Maybelle answered. "When this little lady wakes up, she'll want another lady close by."

So the remainder of the night all four sat beside Amy Jane, Luther nodded and snored, while Maybelle jabbed him in his side. Ray and Jim silently prayed.

The next morning, just about sunrise, Amy Jane began to stir. Jim and the others jumped up and stood by the bed. Slowly Amy Jane opened her eyes and smiled when she saw Maybelle.

"Good morning, little lady," Maybelle said. "Did you sleep well?"

"Yes, ma'am, but now I have a headache," Amy Jane answered. "I guess I slept too hard."

Ray stepped closer to the bed. "How are ya a feelin'," he asked.

Amy Jane grabbed the quilt and pulled it around her neck. Then she looked at Ray with alarm.

"Excuse me, sir," Amy Jane said. "I don't like yo're boldness an' what do ya mean by comin' in my room?"

Then she noticed Jim and Luther. "All of ya men, get out of my room!"

"Now, now, dear, it's all right," Maybelle said trying to calm Amy Jane.

"No, ma'am, it ain't all right. I'm a decent girl. I don't have men in my room. And who are ya, anyway?"

"Something's wrong with her," Ray whispered. "I'll go find the doctor."

"I'm Maybelle, sweetheart. Don't you remember? We were all on the stagecoach together."

"No, I don't remember being on the stagecoach with ya or anybody else."

Amy Jane started to sit up, but a sharp pain in her head caused her to lay back against the pillows.

"What is your name?" Maybelle asked.

"I don't know," Amy Jane said after thinking about the question for a few minutes. "I don't remember my name or anything else for thet matter."

The doctor soon arrived with Ray close behind him.

"Hello, little lady, I'm Dr. Midler. How do you feel this morning?"

"I'm fine, thank ya. I jest have a headache," Amy Jane answered.

"Yes, ma'am, I suppose you do," the doctor said looking at the knot on the back of Amy Jane's head.

"Thet hurts," she cried out as the doctor touched the big lump on her head.

"What is your name, little lady?" the doctor asked.

"I don't know."

"Where are you from?"

"I don't know."

"Do you have any family?"

"I don't know."

Question after question the doctor asked Amy Jane, and each time she replied, "I don't know."

"What's wrong with her," Jim asked with concern.

"It's what we call Amnesia."

"What is that," Maybelle asked.

"Well, it is when a person has had a blow to the head, like this young lady. It makes a person lose all their memory."

"Will it last ferever?" Ray asked.

"No, not usually," the doctor replied. "Sometimes if the person falls, receives another blow to their head, or becomes reacquainted with members of their family and their past, then they can remember. Once they regain their memory there are usually no lingering effects from this type of injury."

"I guess I'm the only one who knows 'bout her past," Ray said.

"Ok," the doctor said, "you must stay with her and try to help her remember who she is. What is her name?"

"Amy Jane," Ray answered.

"Amy Jane," the doctor said turning back to Amy Jane, "do you feel like having something to eat?"

"Yes, sir. I'm really hungry."

"Ok, we will all leave, except Maybelle here. She will help you to dress and then you may come down for a good hot breakfast."

"Yes, sir."

****

The next few days Amy Jane walked around trying to figure out who she really was. Ray would take walks with her or sit on the porch talking with her. He told her all about her family out west and about the family she was going to visit in Atlanta. It seemed nothing he said made her remember who she was.

Each night before she retired for the night Amy Jane prayed that she could remember her name and where she was from. She knew her family must surely be wondering and worrying about her. She could not write them and let them know that she was all right because she didn't even know who they were.

The next morning during breakfast Amy Jane asked Ray, "The family ya said I was on my way to visit - when are they expectin' me to arrive in Atlanta?"

"They were expectin' ya to arrive two days ago," Ray answered.

"Well, won't they be worried?"

"Jim sent word thet the stagecoach had problems an' would be delayed a few days. Once ya are ready to travel, he will send a telegram to the coach house in Atlanta an' they will send word to your people."

"Ok," Amy Jane said quietly.

It had been five days since the stagecoach accident and every morning Amy Jane would sit on the porch of the Inn and wait for Ray. Today she sat on the bench a few minutes then decided to walk across the street to the general store. If she was not on the porch, Ray knew he could find her across the street window shopping.

As she was crossing the street a run-a-way horse pulling a wagon came around the corner. In the rush to move out of the way of the horse, Amy Jane tripped on her skirts and fell to the ground.

Ray was just coming out of the Inn when he saw the horse and wagon. Next he saw Amy Jane trying to move out of the way and then she fell.

"Oh Lord," Ray prayed as he rushed to Amy Jane. "Let her be all right."

When he reached Amy Jane, she was beginning to sit up.

"Amy Jane, are ya all right?" Ray asked kneeling beside her.

"Yes, Ray," she answered. "But my head hurts where I hit the ground when I moved out of the way of the horse and wagon.

"Amy Jane!" Ray exclaimed. "Ya know who I am!"

"Oh, Ray," Amy Jane said, " Yes, I know who you are . Why wouldn't I know you? I practically grew up with ya all of my life."

"Thank the Lord," Ray said. "Thank ya, Lord, fer a run-a-way horse an' wagon."

Chapter Seven

Gable Oaks

Amy Jane and the others recovered from the ordeal of the accident. A few days later they arrived in Atlanta. As they rode through the city to the stagecoach inn, it shocked Amy Jane to see such a big place. When they pulled into the station, Ray helped Jim unload Amy Jane's trunk.

When everything was unloaded, Amy Jane walked over to Jim. "Thank ya, so much, Jim, fer helpin' me after the accident," she said. "God bless ya, Jim."

"Thank ya, Amy Jane," Jim said. "But it's my job to make sure my passengers are taken care of on a trip."

"Please be careful, Jim," Amy Jane said.

"This is my last run," Jim said. "I never want to see another pretty lady a layin' hurt beside the road."

"What will ya do?" Amy Jane asked.

"I'm not sure. I'll probably go back to Savannah. I'm sure I'll be able to find work there," Jim answered. "Where are ya goin' now thet yo're in Atlanta?"

"I'll be a goin' to Gable Oaks where my mama's family lives," Amy Jane replied.

"Thet's a fine place, a mighty fine place," Jim said. "Hope to see ya again, Amy Jane."

"Yes, Jim. Maybe we'll meet again."

As they walked away from the stagecoach, Ray came to Amy Jane. "Amy Jane, this is yo're Aunt Catherine," Ray said as he introduced Amy Jane to a middle aged lady.

"Hello, dear Amy Jane," Catherine said with tears in her eyes. "You look just like Rachel."

"Thank ya, Aunt Catherine," Amy Jane said as she gave her aunt a hug.

"Mama will be so happy to see you," Catherine replied. "She has longed for the day that she would be able to see you again. She loved Rachel and was deeply saddened when she learned of her passing. She wasn't feeling too well this morning, so I told her to rest while we came down to pick you up and take you to Gable Oaks."

"I'm happy thet I am finally here," Amy Jane said.

As they were talking together, another young lady walked over and stood beside Catherine.

"Hello," the girl said. "I'm your cousin, Velvet."

"Hello, Velvet,' Amy Jane answered. "I'm pleased to meet ya."

Amy Jane noticed that she and Velvet were about the same. Velvet was a beautiful girl with a sweet smile.

"We are thrilled to have you come to stay with us," Velvet said smiling. "Since receiving your papa's letter, I have been excited and anxiously waiting for you to come."

"I have been anxious, too," Amy Jane replied. "I didn't think this day would ever come."

"Neither did I," Velvet said smiling. "Grandmother has told us so much about you when you were a small child, before your family left for California."

"I'm so anxious to meet Grandmother," Amy Jane replied.

"Well, she is certainly anxious to see you again," Catherine said.

While the ladies conversed, Ray helped Otis, the black man who had driven Catherine's carriage, load Amy Jane's things. After it was all loaded on the carriage, Ray walked over to where the three ladies were talking.

"Amy Jane," Ray said as he walked over to her. "All of yo're things are loaded on the carriage. I'm leavin' now to find me a room. I'll stop by to send a telegram to Joy Louisa."

"Thanks fer takin' care of me on the trip, Ray," Amy Jane uttered through her mixed emotions. "I'll write home as soon as I get settled."

"Ok," Ray answered. "I promised Maw, Mrs. Ellen an' Joy Louisa thet I would send them a telegram when we arrived safe in Atlanta."

"Ok, an' thanks again, Ray."

Amy Jane walked over to the carriage with her aunt and cousin. She could hardly believe that she, Amy Jane Clarke, was finally in Atlanta, the place where she was born.

Aunt Catherine and Velvet showed Amy Jane different places as they rode toward Gable Oaks. As they rode down the streets of Atlanta, Amy Jane was amazed at the big antebellum homes. This place was totally different from her home out west. Oh, how she wished Joy Louisa was with her.

****

Finally, the carriage turned down a long narrow road. Large stately oak trees lined each side of the road. At the end of the long road stood a beautiful two story house with big columns on the front.

"What a lovely home," Amy Jane exclaimed.

"Thank you," Aunt Catherine said. "Welcome to Gable Oaks. This is the place where your mother and I were born. Mama and Papa have lived here for many years. When my husband, Leon, passed away, I brought Velvet and Agnes here to live."

"I'm sorry, I didn't know Uncle Leon had passed away," Amy Jane said.

"Yes, he passed away five years ago," Catherine said, wiping tears from her eyes. "It still seems as if it was only yesterday."

"We left Atlanta," Catherine continued, "and moved to Charleston, South Carolina. One day while Leon was at work for the lumber company, they cut down a big tree and it fell on him. It killed him instantly"

"We had no family in Charleston, so the girls and I moved back here to Gable Oaks. Mama and Papa are getting feeble, so we decided just to stay with them."

"Whoa!" Amy Jane heard Otis say to the horses as he pulled up in front of the large house.

"Welcome to Gable Oaks," Velvet said.

"Thank you," Amy Jane replied.

As they were getting out of the carriage, the front door of the big house opened. There stood Lela and Doyle Ellis, Amy Jane's grandmother and grandfather. Both were showing their age with hair as white as snow. Although they were elderly, both hurriedly approached the carriage.

"Welcome to Gable Oaks, my lovely granddaughter," Lela Ellis said, reaching for Amy Jane.

"Thank ya, Grandmother Ellis. I'm happy to be here," Amy Jane replied.

"Lordy, lordy, child," Doyle Ellis began. "You are the spittin' image of your dear mama. Lela, don't she look just like our Rachel?"

"Yes, she sure does," Lela said wiping tears from her eyes. "The spittin' image of my precious Rachel."

Otis walked up with Amy Jane's trunk. "Which room does you want Miz Amy Jane to stays in?" he asked.

"Put her things in the room across from my room," Velvet said.

"Yas'm," Otis answered as he carried the trunk up the stairs.

"I'm sure Amy Jane is tired from her trip," Catherine began. "So we need to let her go on up and rest a while before we have our meal."

"Yes," Lela said. "We will talk later, my beloved granddaughter."

"Yes, ma'am," Amy Jane replied, as she gave her grandmother a hug. "Thank ya fer allowin' me to come here."

"Oh, honey, you're, oh so welcome!" Lela exclaimed.

"Come, Amy Jane," Velvet said. "Let me show you to your room."

As the two girls walked up the stairs, Amy Jane stopped in astonishment. There hanging on the wall was a portrait of a young girl in her wedding gown. Amy Jane felt as if she were looking in a mirror.

"That," Velvet began, "is Aunt Rachel, your mama."

"Oh, Velvet," Amy Jane exclaimed. "I *do* look jest like my mama."

"You sure do!"

"How I wish I could've known her," Amy Jane said through tears. "I hope Grandmother Ellis will tell me all 'bout my mama."

"I am sure that she will," Velvet replied.

Amy Jane could hardly turn away from the portrait of Rachel. Standing there beside the portrait made her feel as if she was standing beside her mother. Velvet watched in silence as Amy Jane stood, with tears streaming down her cheeks, looking at the portrait.

Velvet showed Amy Jane to her room. It was a beautiful room of a soft pink with a white spread with dark pink flowers. The white ruffled curtains swayed as the gentle spring breeze blew through the opened windows. Amy Jane had never seen a room so elegant.

"Cozetta will take care of you while you are here," Velvet said. "She will draw the bath water for you after you've had your rest."

"Thank ya, but iffen ya show me where everything is, I can get it."

"Oh, no, Cozetta will do anything that you need to have done."

Amy Jane was accustomed to taking care of herself; however, Velvet had mentioned that Cozetta would be there to do everything. She would even do Amy Jane's hair for her. Amy Jane prayed that she would not become too dependent on Cozetta.

Amy Jane did not realize just how tired she was until she lay on the nice feather bed. She fell asleep a few minutes after her head was on the pillow. When Cozetta awoke Amy Jane, she could not believe that she had slept so long.

"Miz Amy Jane," Cozetta said. "Yo bath water's done ready an' a waiting fo' you, an' de' supper will be served in jist a hour."

"Thank ya, Cozetta. I'll hurry," Amy Jane exclaimed as she rushed to get her clothes.

She found that all of her dresses had been pressed and were hanging up neatly. The bath water was warm and smelled of lilac. Everything was perfect. Amy Jane wanted to stay in the tub of warm water, but she knew she must hurry.

When she walked out of her room, Amy Jane felt refreshed. Velvet was waiting at the top of the stairs.

"Did you rest well?" Velvet asked as Amy Jane walked down the hall.

"Oh, yes," Amy Jane answered. "I didn't know jest how tired I was 'til I laid down on thet feather bed."

"Are you two coming to dinnah?" a girl at the bottom of the stairs said in her southern talk.

"Yes, Agnes," Velvet replied.

"Well, you need to rush up a bit. We should not be late. You know how mother hates for people to be late for dinnah."

"Yes, Agnes." Velvet answered. "You haven't met our cousin, Amy Jane, have you, Agnes?"

"No, but we have no time for introductions now. She has taken far too much time already," Agnes snapped.

"I'm sorry," Amy Jane replied. "I didn't know thet I was a holdin' up supper."

"You're not. Don't pay Agnes any mind. We're not late," Velvet said smiling. "You will find that Agnes sometimes has an attitude problem."

"I'll make sure from now on thet I won't be late fer supper," Amy Jane said in her own country way.

Agnes was a very pretty girl, but was nothing compared to her sister, Velvet, Amy Jane thought to herself. "Lord, help me to know how to deal with Agnes," Amy Jane prayed inwardly.

Everyone around the dinner table was happy to have Amy Jane in Atlanta; that is, everyone but Agnes. From her first glimpse of Amy Jane, Agnes told herself that she would not have anything to do with her cousin. Agnes saw how pretty Amy Jane was and became instantly jealous. She thought that Amy Jane would step in on her "territory" of beaus; no one would do that to Agnes Hester.

After dinner the group gathered in the parlor. They were interested in knowing all about Amy Jane's trip and all about the West. Amy Jane told about her trip and the accident that caused the delay.

"That must have been horrible," Velvet said.

"Yes, it was," Amy Jane answered. "I could not remember anything of my past. I didn't know how long it would last."

"The good Lord was with you, sweetheart," Lela said to her granddaughter.

"Yes, ma'am," Amy Jane answered. "I prayed everyday thet He would help me. An' what was so strange is the day I started rememberin' things. I always sat on the porch waitin' fer Ray to come out an' talk with me. He was so good about tryin' to help me remember things."

"That was sweet of him," Lela said.

"You were about to tell us what happened the day you started remembering thing," Velvet said.

"I walked across the street to the general store. Ray always knew iffen he didn't find me on the porch I was usually at the store. Any way, I was walkin' across the street when a run-a-way horse pullin' a wagon came around the corner. I tried to get out of the way, but stepped on my dress an' fell. I hit my head. When Ray got to me I knew who he was. The hit on the head caused me to remember who I really was."

"That is so strange," Velvet said.

"Yes, it is," Amy Jane replied. "The doctor called it Amnesia."

"Well, I am so glad the Lord helped you through all of this. Now you are well and here with us," Doyle Ellis said.

Amy Jane then told them all about Joy Louisa and her little brothers and sister. For many hours she sat answering questions and telling her new family all about the West.

After retiring for the night, Amy Jane lay in the quietness of her room, thinking of the past few hours. She noticed she didn't talk like Velvet or the others. In fact, Agnes had made several remarks about the way Amy Jane had pronounced some of her words.

"Dear Lord," Amy Jane prayed, "Help me to learn a better way to talk. Help me to say my words the way thet they should be said. I know this ain't something to worry ya with, but I sure would 'ppreciate it iffen ya could help me. Also, Lord, help me to be a friend to Agnes even though she does not like the idea of me being here. Give me the patience I need when I'm around her. Be with my family back in the West. Let no harm come upon them. Thank you Lord fer, I mean, for a safe trip here and for helping me after the accident. Amen."

Chapter Eight

Amy Jane & Grandmother

The next few days were busy ones for Amy Jane. Velvet showed her around Gable Oaks and Atlanta, which she enjoyed very much. Atlanta was totally different from her little "home town" out west. At the thought of "home", Amy Jane felt a wave of home-sickness.

That afternoon when Amy Jane went to her room, she sat down and wrote a letter to Joy Louisa and the family.

Dear Joy Louisa,

I have finally arrived in Atlanta, and it is totally different from the home I left. The houses are big two story houses with big round columns on the front porch. Oh, Joy Louisa, I wish ya could be here with me.

I have two cousins and an aunt that live here with Grandmother and Grandfather Ellis. My cousins' names are Agnes and Velvet and they are so different from each other. Velvet is a very nice girl and she has shown me around some of the places in Atlanta. Now Agnes, she is a different story. How I wish you were here to help me cope with her.

You're not gonna believe what she said to me the first day I was here. She told me me that I had taken too long in getting ready for supper and that I caused "dinnah" (in her

Southern drawl) to be late. Velvet heard Agnes say that and told me I was fine, that supper was just now ready. Velvet told me Agnes was afraid that I would step in "her territory" of beaus. Can you imagine that! Oh well, that's enough on Agnes for now.

The trip here was adventurous for sure! We had to stay overnight in a place called Calvert City. It was a rough place. Did Ray tell you that we had to pretend we were married? I like to have died! The stagecoach driver, Jim Overholt (he sure was nice looking) told Ray that it would be very dangerous if the men knew that I was traveling alone. So when we were in the dining room or when any of those worldly men were around, Jim would call us Mr. and Mrs. Taylor. (You won't be upset will you?) It's funny now that I think back, but it sure was not funny then.

After we left Calvert City, just a few miles up the road the stagecoach overturned. It was really bad. I had a big knot on my head and was out of it for a while. Ray told me that I didn't know who I was or anything. He said the medical name for it was Amnesia. After we went back to and stayed in Calvert City a few days, I was hit by a run-a-way horse and buggy. After that I knew who I was. Ain't that crazy? But I'm back to normal now. Thank the Lord!

Let me tell you about Maybelle and Luther Rutherford. They were on the stage-coach with me. They were so funny. She bossed him around and he let her. She was about as round as she was tall, and he was a little skinny man. They didn't match at all. You would have laughed. They were so funny. She complained the whole trip and he would fuss about her complaining.

Then there was Smokey. He was another passenger. He would fuss with Maybelle constantly. It was some trip, I tell you. I'll tell you more about them when I get home.

My room here is a soft pink with a white spread with dark pink flowers and white ruffled curtains. It's not that "bold tacky stuff." It is the soft stuff that I would pick out!!

I know you will think this is awful, but I have a maid that helps me with my bath water, presses my clothes and fixes my hair. It sure is nice, but help me pray that I don't become too accustomed to it. Her name is Cozetta. She is a sweet girl.

Have you noticed my talking (writing)? I am trying to talk better. Agnes poked fun at the way I said some words, so I'm trying hard to talk like a "city girl". Now don't you laugh!

Grandmother and Grandfather are true Christians. Aunt Catherine and Velvet are too, but I have my doubts about Agnes. Jest, oops, I mean just help me pray for her.

I miss all of you! Tell the little ones that I love and miss them, too. Maybe I won't be here too long, we'll just have to wait and see.

I need to close for now. I'm going up to Grandmother's room and talk with her. I'm sure she will tell me all about my mama, Rachel. Until I return, I'm your favorite sister!

Love Ya!
Amy Jane

After she completed her letter, Amy Jane went to have a visit with her grandmother. Since arriving at Gable Oaks, she had not had the quality time that she desired with Lela Ellis. When Amy Jane walked out of her room, Agnes was walking down the hall.

"Hello, Agnes," Amy Jane said smiling to her cousin.

"I think we need to have a talk," Agnes said in disgust. "Don't think that you are coming here to take all my beaus away from me." Agnes said. "If you have that in mind, then you can just load back on the stagecoach and head west."

Agnes stomped down the stairs, leaving Amy Jane standing in shock. Velvet had just walked out of her room as Agnes finished her comment to Amy Jane.

"Oh, Amy Jane," Velvet said. "I am so sorry for Agnes' actions. I don't know why she is that way."

"It's ok, Velvet," Amy Jane replied. "I'm just sorry that she feels that way toward me. I didn't come to take away any of her beaus; I only came to meet my mama's family. I don't want to cause her any problems."

"Don't worry about her," Velvet began. "She thinks every pretty girl is stepping into 'her territory'."

"I hope that she will see that I'm not here to cause her any problems," Amy Jane said.

Amy Jane continued down the hall toward her grandmother's sitting room. The door was closed, so Amy Jane knocked lightly.

"Come in," a call came forth from the room behind the closed door.

Amy Jane pushed open the door and walked inside. Lela Ellis was sitting beside the window, knitting.

"Come in, my beautiful granddaughter," Lela said.

"Hello, Grandmother. How are you this afternoon?" Amy Jane asked as she sat beside the older lady.

"Oh, as well as any old lady could be, I guess," Lela answered. "What's on your mind little lady?"

"I just wanted to talk with ya. I mean you. I ain't, have not, had any time much with you since I've been here."

"What would you like to talk about?" Lela asked.

"I would like to know all about my mama," Amy Jane replied.

"Your mama was one of the sweetest girls that I have ever known. When she was just a child, her attitude and outlook on life were second to none."

Lela sat there a moment. She seemed to be in another world. Amy Jane could see the faraway look in her grandmother's eyes.

"I remember as if it were only yesterday," Lela began. "Your grandfather was working in the fields and I was preparing his noon day meal when a sharp pain went through my body. I knew it was almost time for my baby. I did not know how long it would be since this was my first child."

"I didn't know that mama was yo're, your first baby," Amy Jane said. "Please forgive me grandmother I am trying to learn to talk proper. Sometimes it is difficult ; but, I feel like I am improving.

"That is quite all right my little granddaughter."

"Yes, she was my first little girl and the best little one too." Lela paused a moment.

Amy Jane, looking at her grandmother, thought of how hard it must have been on her when Rachel left.

Lela continued, "I was so afraid the baby would come before Doyle, your grandfather, came in from the fields. I continued preparing his meal between the pains. Time seemed to stand still. A few minutes passed and I heard ole Sam bark. I knew Doyle was coming in."

"Doyle didn't even get to eat his meal, God love his soul." She paused and laughed. "He told me later, 'You sure picked a good time to have that baby. I was so hungry and I didn't even get to eat.' He was just being playful."

"He hopped on his horse and rode to his mama's house as fast as the horse could go."

"Oh, Grandmother, were ya left alone?" Amy Jane asked.

"Yes, dear, and that was the longest time of my life."

"I can jest, no just imagine," Amy Jane replied. "I'd been slap out of my mind with fear."

"Well, I can say, I wasn't very brave myself," Lela said smiling. "The good Lord helped me through it all. Doyle's mama arrived and little Rachel was brought into this world. She was a beautiful baby and was just as beautiful the last time I saw her."

Tears formed in Lela's eyes. "She grew to be a precious young lady. I remember," Lela continued. "the day John asked to be allowed to call on Rachel. He was a fine boy. His family didn't have a lot of material things, but they sure had the love of God among their family. John was also the oldest of the seven Clarke children."

"Papa has mentioned some of his family to me," Amy Jane said. "He said his papa died when all the children were real young. Then his mama died not long afterwards."

"That's right," Lela agreed. "John was about thirteen when his mama died. The Caldwell family took him to live with them so John could help Mr. Caldwell on the farm. All the other children were taken to an orphan home. No one knows whatever became of them."

"How sad," Amy Jane said.

"As I was saying," Lela continued, "I remember when John came to Doyle one day after the Sunday service. 'Brother Doyle', he said, 'would it be all right with you if I come calling on your daughter, Rachel?' Doyle was always one to joke around," Lela laughed.

"He said to John, 'Well, son, you'll have to do like Isaac. You'll have to work for me seven years.' Poor ole John looked at Doyle and said, 'I'd be glad too, sir, but I'll have to talk with Brother Caldwell.'

"I began to laugh," Lela said, "and told John that Doyle was only joking with him."

"I bet he was glad," Amy Jane laughed.

"Yes, he sure was," Lela answered. "Rachel was the happiest girl in the south. Two years later they were married. Rachel was the most beautiful bride there has ever been. She made her own wedding dress. It was lovely; matter of fact, I still have the dress."

"Oh, Grandmother, could I please see it?"

"You certainly can, my dear child," Lela replied. "After dinner you and I will go up to the attic."

"I would love that," Amy Jane said.

"A year after Rachel and John were married, she had a baby girl. You were just as pretty as your mama had been when she was born. Poor little Rachel had a hard time. She had been sick the entire time she carried you. Before you arrived, we thought several times we were going to lose her."

Lela wiped away her tears and continued, "I was afraid if she ever had anymore children she might not make it. She was so frail after you were born. When they told us they were going to California, I cried for a week. I could not bear the thought of my Rachel leaving and going that far away from me."

"Why did Papa want to go to California?" Amy Jane asked.

"Everyone was talking about how gold had been found. Life in California was better."

Lela then told Amy Jane of the rose bush Rachel had taken with her.

"Oh, yes," Amy Jane exclaimed. "Mama, uh, Ellen, told me all about the rose bush."

"It's all right to call her Mama, Amy Jane. I can tell she has truly been a mama to you."

"Yes, ma'am, she sure has," Amy Jane answered.

"Ok, you tell me what happened to the rose bush," Lela said.

Amy Jane proceeded to tell her grandmother the story Ellen had told of the rose bush.

"It was snowing as we tried to find our way toward the city," Amy Jane began. "Papa made the wrong turn and, instead of going to the city, we went farther into the country. Mama was about to have the baby. Papa pulled the wagon up to the first house we came too, and thet, that was Mama Ellen's."

Amy Jane paused a moment, then continued. "Mama Ellen helped Papa put Mama in the bed. Me an' Joy Louisa went down to Maw Maw Graves' house to stay."

Amy Jane wiped away her tears, then continued. "While Papa was gone to get Maw Taylor, Mama told Mama Ellen 'bout the rose bush. Mama said she would be gatherin' roses in a better land before Papa reached California."

"God love her," Lela said through tears. "If anybody made it to the promise land, my sweet Rachel did."

"Later, Papa gave the rose bush to Mama Ellen to try and keep it from dying during the winter. When spring came, Mama Ellen planted the rose bush beside the front porch. I remember the first rose that came on the little bush."

Amy Jane paused a moment then continued, "It was so beautiful. I ran to tell Mama Ellen about the rose. After it completely opened she cut it off the bush and gave it to Papa. She told him to take me to Mama Rachel's grave and put the rose on it."

"What a wonderful person Ellen must be," Lela said.

"I remember Papa taking me to the grave, although I didn't really know what I was doing. Later, Papa told me what I said at the grave. When I placed the rose on the grave I said, 'Mama, dis wrose is fer ya. It is a boo-tee-ful wrose. Jesus made it so boo-tee-ful jest so I could give it to ya.'," Amy Jane said it the way John had told her she said it the day she put the rose on Rachel's grave.

"My dear Amy Jane," Lela said wiping her tears.

The two sat talking for several more minutes about Amy Jane's home out West, about Ellen and others who lived in Hollow Creek.

Velvet came in to let Amy Jane and Lela know that dinner would be ready in five minutes. Lela and her two granddaughters made their way downstairs to the dining room. Dinner was an enjoyable time for Amy Jane, although, Agnes remained cold toward Amy Jane.

During the course of the meal, Agnes made several rude remarks toward Amy Jane. After one such remark, Catherine reprimanded her daughter.

"That remark deserves an apology," Catherine said to her daughter.

"Yes, ma'am," Agnes answered. "I apologize," Agnes mumbled in a tone that let everyone know the apology did not come from her heart.

"You're forgiven," Amy Jane replied.

The remainder of the meal Agnes did not speak. She only gave resentful glances toward Amy Jane. Inwardly, Amy Jane prayed for Agnes.

After the meal Amy Jane went with her grandmother to the attic. Over in the corner lay a trunk with Rachel's name on it.

"Your mama desired to carry this with her to California," Lela began, "but there wasn't any space on the wagon."

Lela knelt beside the trunk and opened the lid. Inside lay the most beautiful wedding gown Amy Jane had ever seen. This dress was the same wedding dress that her mama wore.

"That is gorgeous!" Amy Jane exclaimed, as she ran her fingers over the lovely satin material.

"Take it out," Lela said.

Amy Jane stood in awe as she raised the dress from the trunk. She held the dress up to her.

"This is lovely."

"Yes, it sure is," Lela agreed. "Rachel wanted to take the dress to California so you could have it when you were married."

"I will wear this with much pride for the one who wore it first," Amy Jane said with tears in her eyes. "If that day should ever come, then I will wear this dress proudly."

"If only my Rachel could be here to see her beautiful daughter," Lela said weeping.

Chapter Nine

The Summer Bar-be-cue

Amy Jane had been with her new family now for several months. She had received many letters from Joy Louisa and Ellen. All the letters asked when would she be coming home. Joy Louisa always wanted to know how Ray was doing and when was the last time Amy Jane had seen him. Amy Jane would laugh every time she read that part of Joy Louisa's letter. In every letter Amy Jane wrote to Joy Louisa, she would always tell her that Ray was doing fine and he was in church every Sunday.

On a warm summer day Amy Jane and Velvet were sitting on the front porch with their grandmother enjoying a cold glass of lemonade that Sadie had prepared for them. Grandfather Ellis had been down to the fields talking with Jack, the head field hand.

"Good afternoon, ladies," he said as he walked onto the porch. "How are all my ladies doing this beautiful hot day?"

"We're enjoying our cold lemonade," Velvet said.

"Would ya like for me to go an' get ya something cold to drink, Grandfather?" Amy Jane asked.

"No, dear. Sadie will bring me a glass of lemonade," Grandfather Ellis said as he sat down beside his wife.

"Oh, yes, sir," Amy Jane replied. She continued to have difficulty having someone to prepare things for her. She was always in the habit of doing things herself.

It seemed as if Sadie had some kind of inner instinct. No sooner than Doyle Ellis had seated himself, Sadie came out with a glass of cold lemonade.

"Thank you, Sadie," Doyle said as the maid gave him the glass of lemonade.

"Yas, sur," Sadie answered.

"Well, Lela," Doyle said after he had some cold lemonade. "We need to start planning for our big summer bar-be-cue."

"You're right," Lela agreed. "It's only two weeks away."

"It sure is. Why don't you and the girls here start planning everything. You'll need to get with Sadie and she can give everyone else orders."

"Would you girls like to help me?" Lela asked.

"I don't know what to do," Amy Jane said, "but I'll be happy to do anything you want me to do."

"Every year," Velvet began, "Grandmother and Grandfather have a big outdoor gathering. We've always called it the summer bar-be-cue. People travel from all around to enjoy the food and fun."

"What do ya do?" Amy Jane asked.

"Well, some people will start coming early on that Saturday morning. Some will come from as far away as Macon. Grandfather will have the bar-be-cue pits fired up with roasting pork and chicken on them."

"What else happens?" Amy Jane asked anxiously.

"Usually all the men will stand around and talk or play horse shoes. The ladies will sit on the porch in the shade and the young people will gather around, play games, sing and just have a good time. The children just run and play. There are so many people to meet."

"Sounds like fun," Amy Jane said.

"Later in the evening, the young people gather under the big oak trees. Some of the guys bring their banjos and we have a big sing-a-long."

"That sounds wonderful." Amy Jane said excitedly.

From that moment and for the next few days, Amy Jane, Velvet and Lela were all busy.

The Saturday of the summer bar-be-cue started as a bright and beautiful morning. The barbecue pits, which had been slowly burning since the night before, were now long troughs of rose-red embers with the meats turning on spits above the embers and the juices trickling down and hissing onto the hot coals. The long picnic tables, covered with the finest of the Ellis' linen, stood under the tall oak trees.

At a distance great enough to keep the smoke away from the many guests were the long pits where the meat cooked. There were also the huge iron wash-pots from which the delicious odors of barbecue sauce and Brunswick stew floated. Many servants were running back and forth with trays to serve the guests.

Over behind the barns lay another barbecue pit to take care of the house servants, the coachmen and maids of the guests. They enjoyed their own feast of hoecakes, yams, chitterlings, and barbecue. Doyle always made sure they had plenty of ice-cold watermelons.

The long driveway to Gable Oaks was full of saddled horses and carriages with guests alighting and calling greetings to friends. Grinning servants, excited as always at a party, walked the horses to the backyard to be unharnessed and unsaddled for the day. Many children, black and white, ran about the lawn, playing hopscotch. Some of them were boasting about how much they were going to eat.

The wide hall, which ran from the front of the house to the back, was swamped with people. The girls in crinolines, bright as butterflies, were going up and down the stairs from the second floor, arm in arm. They would stop to lean over the delicate handrails on the banisters, laughing and calling out to the young men in the hall below them.

In the drawing room were the older ladies, in their dark silks, fanning themselves. They were talking of babies and sickness and who had married whom and why. Otis, the butler, hurried about with trays of tall glasses of cold apple cider and lemonade. He was bowing and grinning as he offered each one something to drink.

Many guests assembled on the sunny front veranda. Amy Jane had never seen so many people at one gathering; but, she suddenly remembered how many invitations she and Velvet had written. There were people from Jonesboro, Fayetteville, Lovejoy, and Atlanta. There were some from as far away as Macon and Savannah.

In the crowd, Amy Jane saw Ray Taylor standing under one of the big oak trees. He was talking with a tall handsome young man. Ray saw Amy Jane and motioned for her to come over to him.

"Amy Jane," Ray said as Amy Jane walked up to where the two men were standing. "This is some gatherin', ain't it?"

"Yeah," Amy Jane answered. "I have never seen so many people at one gathering. Joy Louisa would enjoy this wouldn't she?"

"Yeah, she would," Ray answered. "Amy Jane, I want ya to meet my friend, Lawrence Wiggins. Lawrence this is Amy Jane Clarke."

"Pleased to meet you, Mr. Wiggins," Amy Jane said extending her hand to Lawrence.

"It is indeed my pleasure to meet you, Miss Clarke," Lawrence said with a smile.

"I do hope both of you are enjoying yourselves," Amy Jane said.

"Indeed, we are," Lawrence answered.

"It is such a lovely day for this," Amy Jane said. "I was afraid it was going rain, but the day turned out to be beautiful ."

"Yes, it has, but not quite as beautiful as the young lady standing before me," Lawrence said with a smile and a wink at Ray.

Amy Jane could feel herself blush. At the same time she heard her grandmother calling her name.

"It was nice meeting you, Mr. Wiggins," Amy Jane said. "I must run to find out what my grandmother needs."

"Certainly. Maybe there will be more time for us to talk later today."

As she hurried away to find her grandmother, Amy Jane was amazed at how this Lawrence Wiggins was so forward. *But he sure is handsome,* Amy Jane thought. She had mixed emotions about the man.

"Amy Jane, dear," Lela said as Amy Jane walked over to her grandmother. "I want you to meet a dear friend of mine, Hetty Meaders."

"Pleased to meet you, Mrs. Meaders," Amy Jane said.

"My, my, Lela, this child is the spitting image of Rachel," Hetty Meaders said. "And just as beautiful, too."

"Thank you," Amy Jane said.

"Amy Jane!" Velvet called to her cousin.

"You go see Velvet," Lela said. "I just wanted Hetty to see my beautiful granddaughter."

Amy Jane hurried over to where Velvet was standing with several other girls. *I'll never remember all these people,* Amy Jane thought to herself.

"Amy Jane, this is my friend, Victoria Livingston," Velvet said. "Victoria, this is my cousin, Amy Jane."

"It is good to meet you, Amy Jane," Victoria said. "How do you like the South?"

"Well, it is quite different from the West," Amy Jane said with a smile. "But I'm enjoying my visit."

Several more young girls came and mingled with the group already sitting on the ground under the oak trees. They were giggling and talking about all of the handsome young men who were standing around talking. One of the girls mentioned the two young men standing under another tree. Amy Jane followed their gaze and noticed they were speaking of Ray and Lawrence.

"The young man on the left is Ray Taylor," Amy Jane began. "He's my sister's beau. They will probably be married when he finishes his schooling' here in Atlanta."

"Oh how awful," one of the girls groaned. "He is so handsome."

"Do you know the other young man," another girl asked.

"No, not really," Amy Jane answered. "Ray did introduce the other young man to me earlier. His name is Lawrence Wiggins."

"Now he is what I call hand-s-o-m-m-e!" another girl put in.

Amy Jane stayed with Velvet and the other girls until her grandfather called for everyone's attention.

"The food is prepared and ready to eat," Doyle began. "So if you will all bow your heads we will ask Pastor Waddell to bless the food."

After Pastor Waddell prayed, everyone congregated around the long tables. Amy Jane could not believe how much food had been cooked. She suddenly realized just how hungry she was and began to prepare her a plate of food.

"May I ask you to eat your meal with me?" someone whispered behind Amy Jane.

As she turned, Lawrence was smiling at her.

"I'd love too, Mr. Wiggins," Amy Jane said.

Many of the young men were asking the young ladies to join them while they ate their meals. Amy Jane noticed, as she walked with Lawrence to a spot under the tree, that Agnes glared at her.

Oh, no, what have I done now to upset Agnes, Amy Jane thought. She hoped Agnes did not make a scene here in front of Lawrence. Amy Jane noticed that Agnes talked with several young men and at one time with Lawrence.

Agnes was upset. She thought this Lawrence Wiggins was some handsome man. She hoped he would ask *her* to join him during the meal. Instead, *he* had asked Amy Jane. Agnes was furious.

Amy Jane enjoyed getting to know Lawrence. He told her that he was from Savannah. He was in Atlanta studying to become a lawyer and he had been working with her grandfather on some legal matters. Doyle had invited Lawrence to the bar-be-cue.

"I sure am glad I accepted his invitation," Lawrence said. "It would have been terrible to know that I went through life without meeting such a lovely young lady. And to think, she is Mr. Ellis' granddaughter."

"Oh, Lawrence," Amy Jane laughed.

Many hours later Lawrence said good-night to Amy Jane.

"Miss Clarke," Lawrence said as they walked to the front door. "I do hope we can meet again soon. I must return to Savannah tomorrow, but when I do return to Atlanta, may I call on you?"

"Yes, Mr. Wiggins, if my grandfather gives you his permission," Amy Jane answered.

"I will speak with Mr. Ellis before I leave this place. Good-night, Miss Clarke."

"Good-night, Mr. Wiggins."

Slowly, Amy Jane made her way up the stairs to her room. As she reached the top of the stairs, Agnes came out of her room.

"Well, Miss Goody-two shoes, I hope you are satisfied that you monopolized our guest. You would not allow him to talk with any of the other young ladies. Just wait until Mother hears about this."

"Oh, Agnes, I'm so sorry. I didn't mean to take Mr. Wiggins away from anyone. He asked…"

"Yeah, sure, he asked you to join him. Only because your sister's beau told him to ask you."

With that, Agnes stomped back to her room. Amy Jane did not let Agnes' rudeness upset her, for she, on this summer day, had been struck by cupid's arrow of love.

Chapter Ten

Rumors of a War

Summer soon changed to a cool fall. Along with the cooler weather came the changes of the leaves to a beautiful colorful picture. Everyday, since the summer bar-be-cue, Amy Jane had hoped to see Lawrence again. She received several letters from him, but none told when he would be back to Atlanta.

Not knowing of the letters Amy Jane received, Agnes rejoiced in the fact that Lawrence had not returned to Gable Oaks to call on Amy Jane. Amy Jane tried to ignore the many remarks Agnes roared when they passed in the halls of Gable Oaks. Agnes was totally different from her sister, Velvet. Amy Jane wondered how *real* sisters could be so different.

Winter soon arrived, bringing in the cold northern winds. Christmas season in the South varied from the Christmas season Amy Jane knew in her western home. There was much decorating in Atlanta, along with many parties and festivities. The servants were busy cooking and baking, while the rest of the household attended parties and dinners. Amy Jane had never been to so many parties in her life. Many times she wished Joy Louisa could be there to enjoy the fun, too.

When the men gathered in the parlors after each dinner, there was much talk of the newly elected president, Abraham Lincoln. There were also rumors of a war. Word rapidly spread that South Carolina, which became a part of the Union in 1788, had now voted to leave it, being the first state in the pro-slavery Cotton Belt to do so. Within days after South Carolina removed itself from the Union on December 20, Major Robert Anderson secretly moved his soldiers from Charleston's Fort Moultrie to Fort Sumter.

Although there were rumors of a war spreading, Christmas was a joyous time for Amy Jane. She met many new friends. Velvet always made sure she introduced everyone to Amy Jane. She met many fine young men, but she could never forget Lawrence Wiggins. He had sent Amy Jane a letter just before Christmas, wishing her a very Merry Christmas, and was sorry that he could not join her.

****

On March 3, 1861, as soldiers with fixed bayonets watched from rooftops and along the Capitol plaza, Abraham Lincoln was sworn in as President of the United States. It was a nation that had already been divided by the secession of seven Southern states.

On April 15, President Lincoln, carefully avoiding using the word "war", declared a state of "insurrection" as he issued an appeal for men to volunteer for three months of military service. The president's call for troops came only one day after the fall of Fort Sumter into the hands of the Confederate militia.

Many young men, some who Amy Jane had met, headed out to join the military services. There were many sad young ladies as their beaus left to fight in the war. Some even hastened to marry before the young men left. Amy Jane felt compassion for these young women who might never see their new husbands again. Amy Jane helped Velvet give parties for many of her friends who were marrying before the young men went off to war.

One evening as the family sat around the dinner table, Amy Jane noticed Agnes. She was quiet, yet she seemed happy. Soon after the dessert was served Agnes made her announcement.

"I would like to inform everyone," Agnes began, "that Tom Morgan has asked me to become his bride and I have accepted his offer."

"Agnes!" Catherine exclaimed. "How could you do such a thing? You have not even courted Mr. Morgan properly." You know that is not the proper way for a marriage."

"No one is courting *properly* since the war," Agnes argued.

Everyone sat quietly around the table. Agnes sat looking at her mother.

"You hardly know this Mr. Morgan," Catherine continued. "He has not been calling on you and he is not a Christian. I will not allow this to happen," Catherine demanded.

Agnes sat silently for a moment.

"Mother," Agnes began. "Tom will be leaving to join the military soon. He was coming over tonight to talk with you, but could not come. We *will* be married with or without your blessings."

Agnes pushed her chair back from the table, stood and walked out of the room. There was not a sound made in the room. Everyone sat in shock. Catherine started to go after Agnes.

"Let her be, Catherine," Doyle Ellis said quietly. "She will come to her senses before going on with this."

"I don't think so, Father," Catherine said, shaking her head. "She is determined to marry, like so many girls are doing."

As they sat around the table silently, they heard a knock at the door. Otis announced that a visitor waited in the parlor for Miz Catherine. She slowly walked to the parlor, knowing Tom Morgan was waiting for her.

"Hello, Mrs. Hester," Tom Morgan said as Catherine walked into the parlor.

"Good evening, Mr. Morgan," Catherine answered.

"Ma'am, I have come to ask your permission to marry your daughter, Agnes," Tom said after a few moments of silence. "I know you may think this is a sudden decision, but I have thought about this for quite some time now."

"But, Mr. Morgan," Catherine interrupted, "You have not even been calling on Agnes in the proper manner."

"Yes, ma'am, I realize that," Tom answered. "I was planning on being her caller, but now since the war, I don't have the time to be a proper caller."

"Are you a Christian, Mr. Morgan?" Catherine asked.

"Well," Tom stammered. "No, ma'am, but I have given that much thought, too."

"I can not and will not allow Agnes to marry a man who is not a Christian."

"Yes, ma'am, I understand," Tom said. "Goodnight, Mrs. Hester."

Tom walked out of the parlor and out the front door. Unknown to Catherine, Agnes had been standing outside the window. When Tom walked outside, Agnes met him.

"Agnes, darling," Tom began. "Your mother has forbidden us to be married, so…"

"Tom," Agnes interrupted. "I didn't know that you were coming over tonight. So after dinner, I told everyone that we were getting married. Mother told me the same thing that she just said to you. I told her that we were marrying with or without her blessings. Oh, Tom, darling, I can't let you go away to war without becoming your wife."

"But, Agnes, dear, we can't go against your mother," Tom said putting his arm around Agnes.

"We can go away tomorrow, Tom," Agnes said.

"Yes, I guess we can," Tom agreed. "Meet me tomorrow morning at six o'clock over by the barn. I will have the horse and buggy waiting." Tom kissed Agnes and left.

Agnes made her way back to her room, closed the door and began to put some clothes in a bag. As she was packing her things, there was a knock on her door.

"Agnes, may I come in?" Catherine asked her daughter.

"Really, Mother, I'm tired and have a headache," Agnes said. "I'll talk with you tomorrow."

"Very well," Catherine answered. "Good night, dear. I love you."

Agnes had been afraid that her mother would persuade her to open the door. She knew if her mother came in and found clothes scattered about, she would be very upset. When she heard her mother's footsteps descend down the stairs, Agnes sighed in relief.

Agnes awoke the next morning very early. The night before, she had written her mother a note saying she and Tom would be married and then return later. Before the sun rose in the east, Agnes silently slipped out of the house to meet Tom by the barn.

As he had promised the night before, Tom Morgan was waiting with his horse and buggy. He helped Agnes in the buggy and the two headed toward the city to find someone to marry them.

In her room, Catherine could not sleep. She decided to take a walk in the rose garden. As she passed Agnes' room, the door was open. Catherine walked in the room, saw the bed was made and realized Agnes was not there. It was then Catherine saw the note on the dresser.

> *Dear Mother,*
>
> *I know this will hurt you, but I have left with Tom. We will be married today and will contimue on to Savannah. Tom is to report for service in seven days. That will give us time to be together and make it to Savannah before Tom must report for duty. Please don't be too upset with me. I must do what I feel is the right thing for me and Tom.*
>
> *Love your daughter,*
>
> *Agnes*

Catherine read and re-read the note several times. She sat and cried, knowing Agnes was doing the wrong thing. She also knew Agnes would regret this day later on.

"Lord," Catherine began to pray, "please keep your protecting hand on Agnes and Tom."

****

Within a few days, Agnes had become a wife, and within two months more she was a widow. She was soon released from the bonds she assumed with much haste and little thought. She was never again to know the freedom of her unmarried days. Widowhood had crowded in closely on her marriage, but, to her dismay, motherhood soon followed.

Chapter Eleven

Amy Jane, The Nurse

The South overflowed with excitement and enthusiasm. Everyone knew that one battle would end the war and every young man hastened to join up with the military services before the war should end. Many, like Tom Morgan, hastened to marry their sweethearts before they rushed off to Virginia to strike a blow at the Yankees.

There were dozens of war weddings. There was very little time for the sorrow of parting, for everyone was too busy and excited for sad thoughts or tears. Amy Jane had been busy helping Velvet with parties for her friends who were getting married.

Amy Jane did not know that, from the minute the fighting had begun, Atlanta had been transformed. On one trip into the city, Amy Jane realized that in response to the needs of the war, Atlanta had become a hospital base, a manufacturing center, as well as, one of the South's chief depots for the collecting of supplies and food for the armies in the fields.

Amy Jane felt the need to offer her assistance in the hospital. She thought, as they rode back to Gable Oaks, of all the wounded men that were being brought to the hospital everyday. She would definitely speak to her Grandmother and Grandfather Ellis about her plans.

After dinner that evening Amy Jane told her grandparents that she would like to talk with them. Lela felt sure that Amy Jane wanted to return to her home out West.

Oh how I will miss this sweet girl, Lela thought. She was even more surprised when Amy Jane told them of her plans.

"Oh, dear child," Lela began. "There are so many wounded men being brought to the hospital. It would be so depressing for a young lady like you to do such a thing."

"I'm sure that it would be quite depressing, Grandmother, but I feel I could help in so many ways."

"Yes, sweetheart, I am sure you could, but…"

"Well, Lela," Doyle interrupted. "If our granddaughter wants to help, then we should allow her to do so. If she finds out that she can't take the awful sights of the wounded men, then she doesn't have to return to the hospital."

"Thank you, Grandfather," Amy Jane replied.

"Well, if that's what you are sure you want to do," Lela said.

"Yes, Grandmother, I really want to help."

The following day, Amy Jane found herself walking into the hospital. Seeing the many wounded men lying on cots amazed her. The horrible odor smelled like death. She wanted to turn and run out, but she felt in her heart that she must help.

She made her way to the main office, and there she told the lady behind the desk that she would like to volunteer to be of assistance. Of course, they were more than happy to find someone who wanted to volunteer their time to help with the wounded men.

The lady told Amy Jane what time she needed to report to the hospital the next day. Then Amy Jane was told to go down the hall to the first room on the right; there she would be fitted for a uniform to wear. Down the hall, Amy Jane could hear the cries of the many wounded soldiers.

Early the following day, Otis took Amy Jane into the city to begin her work at the hospital. It was already very hot on the clear morning in June. Amy Jane was quiet as they rode toward the hospital.

"Miz Amy Jane," Otis began. "Is you sho' you wants to do dis?"

"Yes, Otis," Amy Jane replied. "I must help. There are so many wounded soldiers who need help."

"Yas'm," Otis answered. "But it sho' ain't gwine be good fer you to sees all dat bad stuff."

"The Lord will help me, Otis," Amy Jane said.

"Yas'm the good Lawd'll be wiff you."

A few minutes later, Otis stopped in front of the hospital. He helped Amy Jane out of the buggy.

"I'se be back to get you later on dis evenin'," Otis said.

"Thank ya, Otis."

"Yas'm. I'se a be a prayin' fo' you today, Miz Amy Jane," Otis said.

"Please do that," Amy Jane replied.

As she walked up the path toward the hospital, Amy Jane prayed, "Please, Lord, help me. Give me the strength that I need to help these men who are hurtin'."

She made her way to the large room where several wounded soldiers had just arrived. Dr. Hemmingway was checking some of the men. When she saw the terrible sight of the badly wounded men, Amy Jane thought she would faint.

"Help me, Lord, please help me," she prayed.

The day soon came to an end. Amy Jane was weary and tired. Otis was waiting to take her back to Gable Oaks when she walked outside.

There were strands of hair falling out of her nurse's cap. She wiped her forehead as she walked toward the buggy that waited for her. She climbed in, sat down, and leaned her head against the back of the seat. She was totally exhausted.

"God bless you, chile," Otis said.

The two rode in silence all the way back to Gable Oaks. Amy Jane enjoyed the breeze and Otis allowed her to relax. He knew it had been hard for this little chile' today.

When they arrived at Gable Oaks, Velvet ran out to meet Amy Jane.

"Dear, Amy Jane," Velvet said. "You look worn out."

"I'm very tired," Amy Jane answered. "Oh Velvet it is so awful. There were hundreds of wounded men brought to the hospital today. It was so sad."

"You can tell me later," Velvet said. "Right now, you need a good bath and a rest. Cozetta has your water ready. You have plenty of time before dinner will be ready."

Amy Jane slowly made her way up the stairs to her room. Cozetta awaited Amy Jane.

"Miz Amy Jane, I'se done fixed yo' bath water. You jest take yo' time an' r'lax. When yo're ready, you ring de bell," Cozetta said.

"Thank you, Cozetta," Amy Jane replied

Amy Jane sat in the tub of water for a long time. She tried to relax, but every time she closed her eyes she saw the many wounded soldiers. Some were dead and others badly wounded.

Amy Jane did not realize how long she had been in the tub until she heard Cozetta calling.

"Miz Amy Jane, Miz Amy Jane," Cozetta called. "Is you 'bout ready to get out of de tub? It's 'bout time fo' dinnah."

Reluctantly, Amy Jane finished her bath, dried herself, and went to dress. Amy Jane asked Cozetta to put her hair in a chignon, since it was so hot. When Cozetta finished with Amy Jane's hair, she made her way down to the dining room.

"Dear Amy Jane," Lela said when Amy Jane walked into the room. "You sure look tired. Are you feeling all right?"

"Yes, ma'am," Amy Jane answered. "I'm quite tired. As soon as I eat, I think I'll just go on back upstairs. Do you mind?"

"No, dear, not at all. You certainly need to rest," Lela said.

As soon as Amy Jane finished eating her meal, she returned to her room. As she slowly ascended the stairs, she could hardly put one foot in front of the other one.

She undressed, put her night gown on and fell onto her feather bed. Hardly before her head hit the pillow, she was sound asleep. All too soon, Cozetta was standing beside Amy Jane's bed with her breakfast.

"Miz Amy Jane," Cozetta whispered. "It's time to get up, ma'am."

"So soon?" Amy Jane asked rubbing her eyes.

"Yas'm. I'se have yo' breakfast here." Cozetta said. "Is you a feelin' better?"

"Yes, I rested very well," Amy Jane answered.

"Is you gwine back to de hospital?"

"Yes, Cozetta, I must continue what I've started. There are so many wounded men who need help."

"Yas'm, but is you sho' you want to do thet?"

"Yes, I must help."

****

Several months had passed and Amy Jane was still doing her duties at the hospital. She had seen so many men die. It broke her heart to realize that these men were someone's brother, son, husband or papa. Amy Jane thought of her papa and brothers back home in the West. She thought of how her mama would feel if her sons were off somewhere fighting in a war.

So many times Amy Jane would ask herself the question, "Would the war ever end?" She was lonesome to see her family out West, but she also knew that she must fulfill her duties as a nurse.

Chapter Twelve

Grandfather's Meeting

Day after day Amy Jane worked with the wounded men. It was a pitiful sight. There were some without arms or legs and others mangled beyond recognition.

One day as Amy Jane walked through the large hospital room, men on both sides of the room called for her. Some needed water, others just wanted to talk to someone. The men in this particular room were not wounded as badly as the other rooms.

As she walked from bed to bed, she heard one of the men call out to her. The voice sounded familiar, but she did not recognize the man. His head was bandaged and his face was swollen.

"Nurse! Nurse!" he cried. "Please, can I have some water?"

Amy Jane filled a cup with cold water and knelt by the man's bed. Slowly he began to sip the water she gave him. One of his eyes was swollen shut, but with the other eye he looked at Amy Jane.

"You're just as pretty as the first time I saw you," the soldier said.

"I've not seen you before, sir," Amy Jane said. "Didn't they just bring you in?"

"Yes, my pretty little nurse. I can't believe you have already forgotten me, but the way I look now, I'm not sure my own mama would even know me."

"What is your name, sir?"

"I'm Sergeant Lawrence Wiggins."

"Oh, Lawrence! I'm so sorry. What happened? Are you all right?"

"Now, now, one question at a time," Lawrence said squeezing Amy Jane's hand. "I think I'll make it, especially now, since I have a good nurse.

"I will do all I can for you, Lawrence," Amy Jane said.

"I know you will." Lawrence said. "How is ole Ray Taylor?"

"He's doing fine, just staying busy here in the hospital," Amy Jane answered.

"He was studying to become a doctor, wasn't he?"

"Yes and he's getting plenty of training."

"I would say that he is," Lawrence said.

"How long have you been in Atlanta?" Amy Jane asked.

"Well, just two days," Lawrence answered. "Me and my men were transferred up here from Savannah. A good buddy of mine was wounded very badly. Could you find out about him for me?"

"Sure, what's his name?"

"Herbert Custer."

"Was he brought in with you?"

"Yes. Just this morning and he was hurt bad. I think maybe he even lost a leg."

"Oh, I'm sorry," Amy Jane said sadly.

"Yes, it was bad. Herbert was a good fellow."

"I'll go see what I can find out." Amy Jane said.

"Thanks, Amy Jane," Lawrence said giving her hand another squeeze.

As she walked away from Lawrence's bed, Amy Jane prayed, "Please, Lord, touch Lawrence."

It had been quite sometime since Amy Jane had received a letter from Lawrence, now she understood why. He had joined the military. It had been a while since that summer she fell in love with Lawrence. He never came back to Atlanta, but she had received several letters from him. She could never get him off of her mind. She prayed many nights that God would bring him back to Atlanta. She sure hated that her prayers were answered this way. She hated to see him wounded and to meet him in such an awful place; however, joy filled her heart to see him again.

As she walked into the room where the badly injured men lay, Amy Jane saw Ray Taylor beside a soldier's bed. She walked over to see if Ray knew anything about Herbert Custer. When she walked up to the bed, she felt as if she would faint.

The man was screaming out with pain. His right leg was mangled and looked as if it were only hanging on by a piece of skin. Ray was trying to give the man a shot, but the poor soldier was in so much pain he could only toss and scream.

When Ray saw Amy Jane he said, "Please see if you can give this man a shot while I hold him,"

As the medicine took affect, the soldier finally began to relax. Together, Amy Jane and Ray began to work on the man's leg. Many times during the ordeal, Amy Jane felt as if she would black out, yet she knew Ray was depending on her help.

"Do you think that you'll have to amputate his leg?" Amy Jane asked.

"No, I think we got it in time," Ray answered. "This fellow will certainly have a bad limp, but he should be thankful he still has a leg."

"You did a great job, Ray," Amy Jane said, as they finished up with the soldier.

"I could have never made it without your help, Amy Jane. Thank you for helping, but why did you come in here? Don't you normally work in the other room?"

"Yes," Amy Jane answered. "Do you remember Lawrence Wiggins?"

"I sure do. I haven't seen Lawrence in a long time. What made you think of him?"

"He's one of my patients."

"Lawrence? Is he all right?"

"I think he will be all right. His head has a bandage on it, one of his eyes is swollen and his arm is broken. He asked me to see if I could find out about his buddy. They were both wounded today. I was trying to locate Lawrence's buddy when I noticed you needed some help."

"Thanks again," Ray said.

"What is this soldier's name?" Amy Jane asked looking down at the wounded man.

Ray looked at the tag attached to the soldier's arm. "Herbert Custer," Ray read.

"That's him," Amy Jane said. "I'll go and let Lawrence know about his friend."

"I'll come with you. I have not seen "ole" Lawrence in quite sometime."

As Amy Jane and Ray walked to Lawrence's bed he opened his eye. "Well, if it ain't Dr. Taylor!" Lawrence said trying to smile.

"And if it ain't my "ole" friend, Lawrence. How are you "ole" buddy?" Ray asked.

"I think I'm going to live now, since that beautiful nurse has helped me."

"Well, I'm glad to hear that," Ray said.

"Did you find out about my buddy?" Lawrence asked Amy Jane.

"Yes I did. In fact, that is why it has taken me so long to come back," Amy Jane replied. "I was trying to locate Herbert for you when I noticed Ray needed some help with a badly wounded soldier. When we finished with the soldier I asked Ray who the man was. He looked on the soldier's tag and found out it was Herbert Custer."

"Is he alive?" Lawrence asked with concern.

"Yes," Ray answered. "I was afraid that I would have to take his leg off, but with Amy Jane's help, I think he'll be all right. He will have a very bad limp, but at least he'll have both legs."

"Thanks to you both," Lawrence said.

"Well, Lawrence," Amy Jane said. "I need to go home, but, I'll check on you as soon as I come in tomorrow."

"Good night, beautiful nurse," Lawrence said.

When Amy Jane made her way out of the hospital, Otis awaited her as usual.

"Good evenin', Miz Amy Jane," Otis said as Amy Jane walked to the carriage.

"Good evening, Otis," Amy Jane answered. "How's everything at Gable Oaks today?"

"I'se don't know, Miz Amy Jane. Mister Doyle, he done sent word dat he wants to see all us black peoples. Says we gwine have a meetin'. He's ain't neber had a meetin' with us. I'se think something's a goin' on. De war, it's gettin' bad, Miz Amy Jane."

"Yes, Otis, I'm afraid things are gettin' worse."

"De good Lawd's gonna haff to do something or dis is gwine be the end to all of us."

All the way back to Gable Oaks Otis tried to figure out why Doyle Ellis wanted to meet with the black 'peoples'.

Amy Jane wondered herself, why her grandfather wanted to meet with all the Negroes. Were there problems at Gable Oaks? Every servant, maid and footman seemed happy at Gable Oaks.

When they reached Gable Oaks, as usual, Cozetta had Amy Jane's bath water ready for her.

"Miz Amy Jane," Cozetta began. "I'se have yo bath water ready. I needs to hurry, cause Mister Doyle done said us Negroes are havin' a meetin' wiff him after supper."

"Yes, Otis told me about it," Amy Jane said.

"He done said he wants ever'body to come to the parlo'. All us servants gonna come wiff de white peoples for a meetin'. It done sound strange to me."

Amy Jane let Cozetta continue to rattle on about the meeting. She, herself, could not get her mind off Lawrence Wiggins. She prayed over and over for him to recover from his wounds.

As Amy Jane walked down the stairs for dinner, Velvet came out of her room.

"Hello, Amy Jane," Velvet said. "How was your day at the hospital?"

As the two girls walked toward the dining room, Amy Jane told her cousin about Lawrence.

When the dinner was completed and the servants had taken the dishes out to the kitchen, Doyle Ellis reminded the family about the meeting with the servants.

"Is this meeting for everyone or just the servants?" Velvet asked.

"I would like for the entire family to be present along with all the Negroes here at Gable Oaks," Doyle said.

After the dessert was finished, the family made their way to the parlor. Slowly the servants, maids, footmen and field hands made their way to the parlor. Many of the field hands were nervous because they had never even been inside the main house, now they were being invited to come into the parlor.

After everyone gathered in the parlor, Doyle stood in front of the group.

"I would like to thank all of you for coming tonight," he began. "I know you all think this is strange and I must say that it is. We all know that the war is bad and is even getting worse."

He paused a moment then continued, "We also know the reason for the war is to free all of the slaves. As of tonight, all of you Negroes are free. You can stay here and be paid or you can leave and go wherever you want to go. How many of you will be leaving Gable Oaks?"

A few of the field hands raised their hands saying they would leave.

"Ok, those of you that raised your hands, you are dismissed to go pack your personal belongings and leave."

He waited until those who were leaving had left before he continued. "Now, those of you who remain will be rewarded for staying. Not only will you be paid for your work here at Gable Oaks, but you will each be allowed to pick out a parcel of land to build a house for you and your family."

There was much excitement in the room. Then Otis came forward and stood beside Doyle.

"Mister Doyle, I'se like to say somethin'," Otis said.

"Sure, Otis, just say whatever is on your mind."

"I thinks I'se a speakin' fo' all us black peoples in dis room," Otis began. "We's don't 'spect you to give up yo' land to us. You done paid a big price fo' all of us many years ago. We's here to works fo' you, not here to take yo' land."

"Dat's right, Brother Otis," someone spoke up in the back of the room.

"I'se be right her' to help you an' yo' family."

"Thank you, Otis," Doyle said. "I know I can depend on all of you; however, I want each family to pick out a parcel of land and when you are ready to build your family a house, the land will be there for you. So tomorrow, I want each of you to take your family and decide which parcel of land you want to build on."

"Thank you, Mister Doyle. The good Lawd will sho' bless you and yo' family."

As the servants and their families left the room, each came up to shake Doyle's hand and to tell him how much they appreciated him. Amy Jane sat with tears in her eyes as she watched the servants shake their master's hand. Many of them walked out of the room with tears in their eyes.

Chapter Thirteen

The Funeral

Many months passed and it seemed the war would never come to an end. People would often say, "just one more battle and the war will be over."

Everywhere people looked, there were more and more Yankees. They seemed to be taking over everything in Atlanta and the surrounding areas. Everything and everybody had changed. The South wasn't like it use to be.

Amy Jane continued her work at the hospital. There were many times she longed to go home - to her family out West. She thought before she left Atlanta she must first be sure Lawrence and Herbert recuperated. She thought for sure Lawrence would be fine, but she was unsure about Herbert. His leg was healing slowly; furthermore, his spirit was not good.

****

Lawrence had been out of the hospital now for a few weeks. He came everyday to check on Herbert, and would always try to come when Amy Jane would be at the hospital.

As soon as the doctor completely released Lawrence, he returned to battle. The night before he left he came to Gable Oaks to visit Amy Jane. As much as he regretted asking her to wait for him, he knew he must. He thought he could never let her go West without him.

Many times while he resided in the hospital, Amy Jane said that she wanted to go back home to her family out West. So often, while she was telling him that she wanted to go back home, he wanted to ask her to wait for him. He felt he was not being fair to ask a beautiful young lady like Amy Jane to wait for a wounded soldier.

Tonight was different. He was well, although he would have to go back to battle he was still going to ask Amy Jane to wait for him. He prayed all the way to Gable Oaks.

When Amy Jane walked into the parlor that evening she was the most beautiful lady that Lawrence had ever seen. He had seen her at the hospital, but now he saw her in a lavender dress. She looked lovely. As she walked into the parlor, he turned and walked to her.

"Amy Jane, you look so beautiful!" Lawrence exclaimed.

"Thank you. You look nice in your uniform, Sergeant Wiggins," Amy Jane said smiling.

"Let's take a walk before dinner, shall we? The sun is setting and it is a gorgeous evening." Lawrence asked as he took both of Amy Jane's hands into his own.

The two walked hand in hand down the long winding drive leading to Gable Oaks. They walked a while in silence, soaking in the beautiful moment together. Lawrence escorted Amy Jane to a place under a large stately oak tree.

"Amy Jane," Lawrence began. "I realize this is probably not the way or the time I should say this, but I must tell you that I have truly fallen in love with you."

He paused, looking into her eyes, "I know it isn't fair to ask you to wait for me, but will you, Amy Jane? Will you please wait for me to finish my tour of duty with the army before you leave to go home?"

"Oh, Lawrence, I would wait forever if that's what it takes," Amy Jane answered.

"I love you, Amy Jane," Lawrence said as he held her close to him.

"I love you, too, Lawrence," Amy Jane answered.

Several months had passed since the evening Lawrence had asked Amy Jane to wait for him. So many nights she cried and prayed for God to be with Lawrence and to bring him safely back to her. Why do we have to fight a war? Will this war ever end? Over and over Amy Jane would ask herself these questions.

The war raged all around and Amy Jane was afraid to even go to the hospital. Grandmother Ellis had become ill, so Amy Jane decided to stay home. Velvet, Amy Jane and Aunt Catherine stayed close to Grandmother Ellis. Her heart had become very weak. The strain of the war around was more that Lela could handle.

One morning as Lela lay on her bed she whispered to Amy Jane, "My dear, Amy Jane, thank you for coming to Atlanta. I longed for many years to have you near me."

She squeezed Amy Jane's hand, then continued, "I am sorry you are in the midst of a war and can't go back to your family in the West. When the war is over, promise me that you will go back to your family. They love you, too."

"Yes, Grandmother," Amy Jane replied. "I will go home just as soon as I can."

"I won't be here much longer, dear child," Lela was saying, "I'll soon be with your sweet mama, my dear Rachel."

"Oh Grandmother," Amy Jane said with tears flowing down her cheeks.

"Don't weep, dear child. I'm ready to go, I am so tired. I can't take this war much longer. I pray the good Lord will take care of all of you," Lela said.

Velvet and Aunt Catherine entered the room with a tray for Lela. Doyle had been busy gathering the valuables of Gable Oaks. Word had spread that the Yankees were going through homes gathering anything of value.

He gathered all the silver, china, any old family heirlooms and took them out to bury them. In the event the Yankees did come, there would not be any valuables for them to take with them. He buried the valuables under the woodshed.

The ladies were sitting around Lela's bed while Aunt Catherine was reading from the Bible. Neither knew, as Aunt Catherine read the Bible, that a Yankee soldier was down stairs going through the kitchen. A few minutes later, the door to the bedroom opened and there stood a tall Yankee soldier.

Each lady, stiff with shock, sat looking at the Yankee soldier. It seemed as if all of time had stopped. Lela, propping up on her elbow, looked at the soldier.

"Could we help you, son?" she asked in a weak voice.

"Yes, I've come for all your silver and gold. Where do you hide it?" he asked in a gruff voice.

"I have no treasures here on this earth hid anyway," Lela began. "All my treasures are laid up in a different place."

"Where? Where are your treasures, ma'am?" the soldier demanded. "If you don't tell me I will search this house until I find them."

"Sir, my treasures are laid up in heaven," Lela said, then fell back on her pillow.

"Oh Mother," Catherine cried as she leaned over Lela.

Amy Jane and Velvet hugged their grandmother as they both wept. The soldier standing in the doorway watched as the three ladies stood by the bedside of someone they loved.

The soldier's mind went back several years to a little farm house in Ohio. He could see his own mother as she lay on the bed. He had just told her that he would be going away to fight for the Union. Having a weak heart, his mother could not take the strain of loosing her only son.

As he stood there, the three ladies, that the soldier saw, were his three sisters as they wept for his own mother. Slowly, the Yankee soldier turned and walked out of the house.

****

Neighbors came to show their respect to a wonderful lady, Lela Ellis. Agnes arrived the day before the funeral, along with Samuel, her small son. Amy Jane felt compassion for Agnes. She was now alone to raise the son of a fallen soldier.

As she sat listening to the preacher, Amy Jane thought of a funeral she had attended as a young child. She didn't know if she really remembered it or if it was the story told to her that she remembered. What she did know was that now Grandmother Ellis rejoiced with her daughter - Amy Jane's mama - Rachel.

Chapter Fourteen

The Yankees Are Comin'

After his wife's death, Doyle Ellis seemed to walk around in a daze. There were days when he would sit in the parlor talking to Lela as if she were sitting there beside him. Then other times he would talk about Lela and her funeral. It seemed his mind would come and go.

Amy Jane felt so sorry for her grandfather. He and Lela had been very close and it was hard for him to give her up. It was hard enough losing his wife, but things were getting bad around Gable Oaks. The Yankees had taken almost everything, including food and cotton.

There were three cows left in the field, a few hogs and some chickens. The cows were needed for milk for Agnes' small son. Otis had buried some sweet potatoes earlier. Things were really looking bad.

Since Lela's death, Doyle was not the same. He seemed to have given up on living. Amy Jane tried talking with him, but he only answered when asked questions. He always sat in Lela's sewing room, now, in her favorite chair, looking out the window. Amy Jane was saddened to see her, once strong, grandfather fading away.

One cool autumn morning Amy Jane went to check on her grandfather. There in Lela's favorite chair sat Doyle with his head leaning on the back of the high-backed rocking chair. Amy Jane walked over and laid her hand on Doyle's arm as she knelt beside the chair.

"Grandfather, yo're breakfast is ready," Amy Jane said.

Doyle did not move. Amy Jane put her hand over his wrinkled hand. It was cold and hard.

"Aunt Catherine," Amy Jane cried out in horror. "Come quick, something's wrong with Grandfather."

Catherine rushed in with Velvet close behind her.

"He's gone," Catherine cried. "God love him. He's not been the same since Mama left us. He's finally with her and Rachel."

Amy Jane wept.

The day of Doyle's funeral was cool yet clear. The neighbors, those who were still around, came to show their respect for Doyle Ellis. Sadie cooked what she could round up for the family to have after the funeral. There wasn't much left, but Sadie did what she could with what she had.

She was thankful that none of the neighbors came over after the funeral. Sadie reminisced about the free hearted Mister Doyle. She thought about how when the war first began, he called all the slaves in for a meeting. Some left Gable Oaks that night, others stayed and were given land of their own to build and live on when the war was over.

Everyone thought then that the war would not last long; but now, three years later, the war was worse than ever. Sadie thought of the land that Otis had picked out for their family. He was going to build Sadie a nice house - "when the war was over," Otis had said. *Will this war ever end?* Sadie thought.

When the family came home from the funeral of their beloved Doyle Ellis, sadness still filled their lives . The man, who at one time had been the strong leader of Gable Oaks, now lay beside his dear wife in the family cemetery. As they sat around the big table, Catherine asked Otis and Sadie to join the family for the meal.

"No'm, us Negroes don't sat at the table wiff de white folks," Otis said.

"Otis, you and Sadie are a part of our family, you're not slaves anymore. Papa freed you three years ago, but you stayed. You are the only man in the house now, so I'm asking you to set in Papa's place and Sadie in Mama's place."

"Oh, Miz Catherine, I'se not worthy to sit in Mister Doyle's place," Otis said with tears in his eyes.

"Please, Otis, will you do it for me? We don't know how long this cruel war will continue, so let's have a meal together in memory of Mama and Papa. They considered you a part of the family."

"Yas'm," Otis said quietly, nodding for Sadie to be seated in Lela's chair.

When they were seated, Otis lead the family in prayer. When he was completed there was not a dry eye around the table.

The next day, a mid-November day, they sat around the dinner table for the noon day meal. Otis had gone out earlier that morning to milk the cows and to check on the hogs and chickens. He had been busy and not joined the ladies with their meal.

There was a chill in the air, the first chill of the year They finished the last of the dessert prepared by Sadie from corn meal and dried huckleberries, sweetened with sorghum and then Otis walked in with a bucket of milk.

"Ain't it 'bout time fer de hawg killin'?" he asked rubbing his hands together.

"You can taste those chitlins, can't you, Otis?" Catherine said with a smile. "I can taste some fresh pork myself, and if the weather stays this cool for a few more days, we'll.."

Agnes interrupted, "Listen, mama, somebody's coming."

"Somebody's a hollerin," Otis said uneasily.

Through the crisp fall air came the sound of horse's hooves thudding as swiftly as a frightened heart. Then came a woman's voice, high pitched, screaming, "Catherine! Catherine!"

A look of horror as eye met eye for a dreadful second around the table before chairs were pushed back and they all jumped up. Despite the fear that made it so shrill, the voice they recognized was that of Eloise Walden. She had stopped by Gable Oaks, only an hour before, for a brief chat with Catherine. She had decided to go see the new Carlton baby.

With Otis leading the way, they all rushed to the front door. They saw Eloise coming up the drive, like the wind, on a lathered horse. Her bonnet dangled by its ribbons and her hair was streaming behind her. As she galloped madly toward them, she began to wave her arm back in the direction she had just come from.

"The Yankees are coming! The Yankees are coming! I saw them! Down the road! The Yankees are coming!"

She swung the horse around just in time to keep him from leaping on the porch. The horse and rider turned around and in four strides were across the side lawn. Eloise put the horse across the four foot hedge as if she were on the hunting fields.

They heard the heavy pounding of the horse's hooves as he carried the terrified rider through the back yard and down the narrow lane between the cabins of the quarters. Eloise trekked across the fields and headed for Oakdale.

For a moment they stood paralyzed in shock, but then Velvet and Amy Jane began to sob and clutched one another. Catherine thought of the few things they did have and knew she would do anything to keep the Yankees from getting it.

"They will not have them!" Catherine cried aloud.

They all turned and faced Catherine. They feared her mind had snapped under the pressure of the things that had happened.

"I will not go hungry! They will not have them!"

"Have what, mama? What is it?" Velvet asked.

"The cows! The pigs! The apples and yams! The chickens! I will not let the Yankees take them from us!" Catherine screamed hysterically.

She turned swiftly to the four Negroes who huddled in the doorway. Their black faces looked peculiarly ashen.

"The swamp!" she said rapidly.

"Whut swamp?" Carl asked.

"The river swamp," Otis said to his son.

"All of you! Quickly get to moving!" Catherine demanded. "Carl, you and Cozetta go get the pigs. The cows are already down there, right Otis?"

"Yas'm"

"Velvet, you and Amy Jane fill the baskets with as much food as you can carry and get to the woods. Agnes take your son and head for the woods. Now! Don't just stand there, take the boy and leave! Sadie, you go put the silver in the well again."

Doyle had buried the silver once before, but they had used it again since that time. After using it they had buried the silver in the well. Just yesterday, Sadie used the silver for their dinner after Doyle's funeral.

Everyone ran in different directions.

"Otis, go get the horse and take him to the river swamp."

"Yas'm," Otis answered.

Catherine noticed that Otis stood still.

"Otis, the horse needs to go!"

"Yas'm, but I'se ain't gwine no whur's til you comes too. You says I'se de man of de house, dat's whut I'se gwine to be. You goes on to de woods wiff de others. I'se gwine make sho' all is well, den I'se come on wiff de horse. Now goes on Miz Catherine. I'se won't leave you herah!"

Catherine ran through the house gathering food and anything else that she could carry. Velvet and Amy Jane filled their baskets.

"Let's go girls. We don't have much time."

The three headed for the woods.

Otis went through the house to make sure everyone was out. He saw a bag of apples and picked them up, then started out the door. As he ran toward the barn to get the horse, he heard the sounds of the Yankees coming. Just as he headed for the woods, a shot was fired. Otis fell to the ground and the horse ran wildly. Some of the Yankees finally captured the horse and others went through the house.

Sherman was marching through Georgia from Atlanta to the sea. Atlanta lay in smoldering ruins behind him and his troops. After months of shelling and nearby battles, Atlanta had become an inferno.

Now inside Gable Oaks, the Yankee soldiers were turning over furniture, breaking china and mirrors, searching for valuables. The men came rambling into the hall from upstairs and from the outside.

"Find anything?" the sergeant questioned.

"A few chickens and a bag of apples," one soldier answered.

"We got us a good horse," another said. "Had to shoot a slave, but we got it."

"We got some corn and a few sweet potatoes and beans," another one said. "That wildcat we saw up the road on that horse must have given the alarm, all right."

"A Paul Revere, eh?"

"Well, there ain't much here Sarge. Let's move on before the whole country finds out we're coming."

"Did you dig under the smokehouse? They usually bury things there."

"Ain't no smokehouse."

"Did you check in the slave's cabins?"

"Nothing but cotton in the cabins, we set fire to them."

"Ok, men, let's go."

"You want us to set fire to the house?"

"No," the sergeant answered. "Leave it be."

He had realized this was the very house he had been through before. This was where the lady said she had her treasures buried in heaven. The Sergeant recalled how the woman had laid back against her pillow and died. Again, the scene from his Ohio home came before him as he saw his own mama die.

"Hey, Sarge, you ain't gettin' soft on us are you?"

"No! I said to travel on and that's what I mean. Leave this house as it is and NOW!"

The soldiers scrambled out the door and on down the road to search another home.

Chapter Fifteen

The Rebuilding

Out in the woods, everyone huddled together. Sadie cried softly because she saw Otis fall from the horse. Carl was going to his papa, but Sadie held to her son's arm.

"No, Carl, dem Yankees will kill you," Sadie cried.

Reluctantly, Carl sat down. He put his face in his hands and wept bitterly. Amy Jane sat beside Cozetta, who wept as well.

"We need to pray," Velvet said.

"Oh, God," Agnes yelled, "the house is on fire."

"No dear," Catherine said, "it's not the house but one on the cabins. I prayed they would spare the house. Let's pray!"

The group huddled together and began to pray. After, hiding for what seemed like forever, they decided the Yankees had traveled on down the road. As they started toward the house, there on the path, lay Otis. The group of ladies and Carl knelt beside him. Amy Jane, having helped out in the hospital, began to check Otis.

"Sadie!" Amy Jane screamed out. "Otis ain't dead! Let's get him to the house."

"Thank you, Lawd. Thank you, Lawd! Sadie cried "Whut do we need to do, Miz Amy Jane?"

"Carl, you help me carry him into the house," Amy Jane began. "Sadie, you go boil some water. Velvet you see if you can find something to use as bandages. Aunt Catherine prepare one of the beds."

"Honey, chile, you ain't qwine be able to tote my Otis," Sadie said.

"Ok, Cozetta, you help me and Carl," Amy Jane said.

"Yas'm," Cozetta answered.

Carrying Otis between them, the three slowly made their way to the house. It was a hard and heavy task for Cozetta and Amy Jane. Both were small girls, but they knew they must do what had to be done.

When they finally reached the house, everybody had performed the task that Amy Jane had ordered. The house itself was a disaster. Tables were turned over, mirrors broken and everything ransacked.

As soon as they laid Otis on the bed, Amy Jane began to clean the gun shot wound. The bullet did not lodge in Otis. It had made a terrible looking wound, but Otis would be fine. He broke his leg and arm from the fall.

Amy Jane was thankful Otis had been knocked out. She didn't have anything to give him, so she must work fast. With the help of Velvet, Amy Jane bandaged Otis before he awoke.

He began to groan just as Amy Jane placed the last bandage on his arm. She knew the Lord had answered her prayers by letting Otis stay unconscious until she completed her task.

As the day slowly ended, the cool breezes of the night appeared. There wasn't much firewood so they all gathered in the one room where Otis lay. Carl collected as much firewood as he could find. Just before darkness set in Catherine went throughout the house to find some candles.

During the night Sadie sat on one side of Otis' bed and Amy Jane sat on the other side. Otis began to groan and tried to turn in his bed.

"Now, now, dear," Sadie said. "You just lay still. You done been shot by dem Yankees."

"Dem Yankees!" Otis said. "Dey gwine to face de Lawd one of des days fo' dis an' all de other thangs dey done to all de peoples."

"Yes, yes, you jest be calm fo' now," Sadie said.

All during the night Otis talked about the Yankees 'a comin'. Amy Jane bathed the fevered brow of the old black gentleman. Just as the new day dawned, Otis started talking again.

"Lawd, have murcy," Otis began. "I sho' nuff had me some bad dreams. I dreamt…" Then he realized he wore some bandages. "Dey wun't bad dreams. Dis is very much real."

"Yes, Otis," Amy Jane answered. "You were shot by the Yankees as you headed to the river swamp on the horse. The bullet didn't lodge in you, but it did give you a bad wound."

"And you fell off the hoss an' you done broke you lagg an' arm," Sadie was saying. "Dis sweet chile here put all dem bandages on yo' arm an' lagg."

"God bless you, Miz Amy Jane," Otis said. "Dey didn't burn de house down?"

"No, but dey went through all de stuff," Sadie answered.

"Well, 'least we has a roof ober our heads."

****

The following April, General Johnston surrendered in North Carolina and the war was over. It was not until two weeks later that the news reached Gable Oaks. There was too much to be done at Gable Oaks for anyone to waste time traveling around listening to gossip. All the neighbors were just as busy as the ones at Gable Oaks, so there was little visiting; therefore, news spread slowly. The cruel war left broken homes and dead and wounded bodies everywhere.

Otis had begun the spring plowing. The cotton and garden seed that Carl brought from his trip to Macon were being planted. Carl told of his trip to Macon and how that many times he narrowly escaped. He traveled down the country lanes and the bypaths to avoid the yankees.

Everyone at Gable Oaks welcomed Carl home, along with his wagon load of seed, fowls, side meat, ham, meal, and dress goods. It was good to have some "real" food again. Sadie, although free, still wanted to cook for the family at Gable Oaks.

Otis began building a house on the land Doyle Ellis gave him before the war had taken a turn for the worse. He and Carl also helped Catherine with the re-building of Gable Oaks. There was plenty of work for every pair of hands.

The withered stalks of last year's cotton had to be pulled up so this year's cotton seeds could be planted. Weeds had to be removed from the garden and the new seeds planted. Firewood had to be cut. Fences burned by the Yankees had to be replaced.

There were floors to be swept, beds to be made, food to be cooked, dishes to be washed, hogs and chickens to be fed and eggs to be gathered. Everyone had their duties, even Agnes' little son. Everybody worked together to re-build the things that had been torn down by the war.

The war is over, Amy Jane thought to herself one day as she washed the dishes. *Now I can go home!* Then in her thoughts came Lawrence. She had not heard from him in a while. *I must find out about him,* she thought. *I promised him that I would not go back West until he returned.*

Was he alive? Was he a prisoner in the Yankee's jail somewhere? Would he ever be able to return to her?

Chapter Sixteen

Captain Lawrence Wiggins

Spring changed to a hot southern summer. Amy Jane had received a letter from Joy Louisa. Since the mail was slow during the war, Amy Jane had not heard from her family out West very often. It was always good to hear that everyone out West was doing fine.

As she read and reread Joy Louisa's letter there was a lonesome feeling within Amy Jane. She longed to return to her western home. It had been almost five years since she had left her family to come to Atlanta. Amy Jane prayed daily that she would receive a letter from Lawrence.

He had not written since before the war ended back in April. Amy Jane had received several letters from him since the day he rejoined his company, after his hospital stay. Although Amy Jane wanted to return West, she longed to see Lawrence. With every letter she had received from him, she knew she loved Lawrence more and more.

In the last letter, he had written that he could hardly wait to be able to return to Atlanta. That letter came in March. He had mentioned that he was in the heat of the battle. Amy Jane prayed he would not be wounded again.

Things at Gable Oaks were *almost* normal again. The gardens were producing vegetables; there was real food. Things would never be the same without Grandmother and Grandfather Ellis at Gable Oaks.

Amy Jane sat on the large porch of the big white house writing to Joy Louisa. In her last letter Joy Louisa had written that Ray had plans of returning West in a few weeks. The family hoped Amy Jane could return with Ray.

Now as she sat writing her letter Amy Jane knew that she must tell her family more about Lawrence. She had mentioned him in several letters and had written more about him in her letters to Joy Louisa; however, she still had not told them the real reason she could not return home. She must first hear from Lawrence before she could make her final decision.

As she sat "day-dreaming", in the distance she saw a cloud of dust. *Someone must be coming to visit Gable Oaks*, Amy Jane thought. As it came closer, she noticed a big black horse with a lone rider. Her heart leaped within as she noticed the man on the horse was Lawrence.

"Calm yo'self," Amy Jane said aloud.

She stood and walked to the edge of the porch. The horse had hardly come to a halt when Lawrence jumped off.

"My sweet Amy Jane," Lawrence said rushing to her. "You are so beautiful!"

He took both of her hands into his hands, held them for a moment, as he looked into Amy Jane's eyes.

"Oh, Lawrence, it is so good to see you," Amy Jane said through tears of joy. "I have been so worried about you."

"Everything is fine now," Lawrence began. "I have finally arrived. I have longed to see your beautiful face. In the heat of the battle the only thing that kept me going was the image of your pretty face in my mind and the hope of seeing you again one day."

The two, holding hands, walked over to sit on the porch.

"I am sorry I haven't sent you a letter since March, but I was not allowed to," Lawrence said.

"What do ya mean, Lawrence?" Amy Jane asked in alarm.

"Well, I was captured by the Yankee army when Sherman made his way through Savannah. You remember Herbert Custer, don't you?" Lawrence asked.

"Yes. He was the one who was wounded very badly when you were in the hospital in Atlanta, right?"

"Yes, well he and I were both captured together. I had just made the rank as Captain. The Yankees killed everyone else in my company. For some reason or other they took me and Herbert captive."

"Oh how awful," Amy Jane exclaimed.

"But now, that's over," Lawrence said smiling. "I'm back with you."

"How is Herbert?" Amy Jane asked with concern.

"I don't know," Lawrence said shaking his head. "He tried to escape, but they captured him and put him back in prison."

"How sad," Amy Jane said.

"Yes, it is," Lawrence agreed. "Ole Custer was a good soldier. I've seen him many times help his fellow comrades."

Velvet came out on the porch.

"Hello, Lawrence," Velvet said. "I thought I heard someone ride up. You'll be staying for dinner won't you?"

"If it won't be any problem, I would love too," Lawrence answered.

"Not a problem at all," Velvet replied. "I'll go and let Sadie know to prepare a place for you."

"Thanks," Lawrence said. "Is Sadie still the cook here?" Lawrence asked Amy Jane after Velvet had returned inside the house.

"Yes. Sadie, Otis, Cozetta and Carl are still a part of Gable Oaks. Grandfather gave each slave family a plot of land before he died. All the others either left before the war got too bad or during the war. Otis and his family stayed."

"Now that's what I call loyalty," Lawrence said.

Amy Jane then told Lawrence about the day the Yankees came through Gable Oaks.

"We just knew Otis was dead," Amy Jane said.

"If it had not been for this pretty little nurse, he would have died," Lawrence said.

"The Lord sure helped me do what needed to be done for Otis. You know," Amy Jane continued, "we still don't understand why they didn't burn the house."

"The Lord was with you and your family."

"Yes, he sure was," Amy Jane agreed.

After dinner Lawrence asked Amy Jane to take a walk with him. Slowly they walked down the lane of Gable Oaks. Lawrence led Amy Jane to the big oak tree they had stood under the night before he left to rejoin his company.

"Do you remember this oak tree, Amy Jane?"

"Yes, I sure do," Amy Jane replied. "You'll never know how many times I walked down and stood under this tree, reminiscing about that day."

"Yes, it seems like ages ago," Lawrence said. "And you'll never know how many times, lying under the stars in the Yankee's camp, that I relived those precious moments. Many times I didn't know if I would ever stand under this tree with you again."

"Oh, Lawrence," Amy Jane said. "I'm so glad the Lord brought you back."

"So am I," Lawrence answered. "So am I."

The two stood there looking at the lovely sun set. As they stood, each thinking of the other, absorbing this moment together, slowly the stars began to twinkle.

"Amy Jane," Lawrence began. "What are you planning to do? Are you going back to your home out West?"

"I would love to go back," Amy Jane answered. "It's been a long time since I've been home."

Lawrence was quiet for a few minutes. Amy Jane thought she had said the wrong thing. *Maybe he didn't want to go West, but she must go see her family. Surely he understood that,* she thought.

Lawrence suddenly broke the silence. "Star light, star bright, wish I might get the wish I wish tonight," Lawrence said, looking up to the star-lit heavens.

"And what might that wish be?" Amy Jane asked laughing.

Lawrence put his hand on Amy Jane's shoulder and turned her to face him. Looking at Amy Jane, Lawrence said, "That you, Amy Jane Clarke, would become my wife. Will you marry me, beautiful Amy Jane?"

"Yes, Lawrence," Amy Jane said smiling. "I have waited for you throughout the war, not knowing if you would ever come back."

Lawrence drew Amy Jane close to him, lifting her face, he kissed her gently.

"Amy Jane, I love you," Lawrence said.

"I love you, too," Amy Jane answered.

Chapter Seventeen

Lawrence Writes A Letter

Lawrence and Amy Jane were both excited. After making their plans, they went back to the house to tell the news to everyone at Gable Oaks. Amy Jane was bubbling inside and could hardly wait to write to Joy Louisa.

Velvet and Catherine were sitting on the porch when Amy Jane and Lawrence walked to the house. Catherine noticed the glow on Amy Jane's face and the twinkle in Lawrence's eyes.

"Isn't this a beautiful night?" Catherine asked as the couple walked up to the porch.

"Yes, ma'am," Amy Jane said smiling. She wanted to blurt out the news, but knew that would not be proper.

"Yes, ma'am, now that you've mentioned it, it is a beautiful night," Lawrence said grinning. "I haven't noticed the night, I've only noticed this beautiful lady that I've asked to become my wife."

"Oh, Amy Jane," Velvet said, rushing to her cousin's side. "I am so happy for you!"

The two girls hugged each other.

"That is wonderful," Catherine said also giving her niece a hug. "And when did this happen?"

"Well, in my mind, several months ago," Lawrence said, laughing. "But in reality, just a few minutes ago."

"I am indeed happy for the two of you," Catherine said. "Does this mean you will soon leave us?"

"Yes, ma'am," Amy Jane replied. "I want to go back home for my wedding."

"I can understand that," Velvet said. "I would certainly want to have my wedding where *my* family would be."

"We've decided to be married this fall," Amy Jane was saying. "Probably, November. That will give us about five months to get everything planned and buy the train tickets."

"Will that be enough time for you to prepare for a wedding?" Catherine asked.

"I think so," Amy Jane replied. "We are planning on leaving Atlanta the last week of August, if we can get a train ticket. By the time we get home, I'll have about two months to prepare everything."

"Yes, that will be plenty of time. You will have Ellen and Joy Louisa to help you," Catherine answered, with the sound of disappointment in her voice.

Amy Jane noticed that her aunt seemed disappointed all of a sudden.

"Aunt Catherine, would you be so kind as to help me start with the planning for the wedding?"

"Well, dear, if you would like for me too."

"Oh, please, Aunt Catherine. You know all about weddings, I'm sure. I could have everything planned out before I even start home.

"I'm sure you would want to wear Rachel's wedding dress, wouldn't you?" Catherine asked.

"Oh yes, ma'am!" Amy Jane exclaimed. "I would not think of wearing any other dress."

"We will need to make sure that the dress doesn't need to be altered," Catherine was saying. "I don't think that it will, but that task can be taken care of before you leave Atlanta. Then once you reach Hollow Creek, your dress will only have to be hung out so the wrinkles will fall out."

"Yes, ma'am," Amy Jane answered.

"Now we'll need to do this... and we'll need to do this..." Catherine went on. "Now let me go and find..."

When Catherine went into the house, Velvet said laughing, Mama will have it all done for you."

"Yeah, she seemed disappointed when I told her that I was going back home for the wedding," Amy Jane said.

"Yes, but maybe by helping you, she won't be too disappointed by not being able to attend the wedding."

"Not attend the wedding!" Amy Jane asked in alarm. "Oh Velvet, all of you must go West with me for the wedding."

"Are you sure, Amy Jane? We're not a part of the family out West," Velvet said.

"But you're a part of me!" Amy Jane exclaimed. "I must talk with Aunt Catherine about this. All of you *must* go."

"We'll talk about it later," Velvet said. "I'll go in and see if Mama needs help finding whatever she is looking for."

Amy Jane and Lawrence sat on the porch a while longer making plans to travel West. Lawrence needed to go back to Savannah, which Amy Jane dreaded. Both Lawrence's parents had died during the war - his father in battle, and his mother when she learned of her husband's death.

"I need to go back to Savannah to clear up some things about my father's plantation, or what's left of the plantation," Lawrence was saying. "I can sell the land and that will give me money to set up my law practice in Hollow Creek, if there's a need there."

"Oh, I'm sure there'll be a need of a good lawyer,' Amy Jane said. "From the letters I've received from home, Hollow Creek is really growing. Ray plans to set up a doctor's office once he returns."

"We'll just pray I will be able to set up a law office there," Lawrence said.

"I know that Papa will give us some land to build on," Amy Jane said.

"I do wish that I could ask your papa for your hand, the proper way," Lawrence said.

"I know, but Papa will understand," Amy Jane said.

"But how can I ask him?" Lawrence asked. "He needs to know before we arrive in September."

"Yes," Amy Jane replied. "Why don't you write him a letter? You can ask him the proper way in a letter."

"Well," Lawrence laughed. "That won't be the real proper way, but I guess it will be the best way."

"And the only way," Amy Jane laughed.

"I'll write to your papa the first thing tomorrow, get it posted and on its way to Hollow Creek," Lawrence said. "Then I will head on back to Savannah."

"So soon?" Amy Jane asked.

"Well the sooner I get everything settled, the sooner I'll be able to come back to Atlanta. Then we'll be able to prepare for the trip west."

"Yes, I guess so," Amy Jane said sadly. "But you finally come back and now you're leaving again."

"I'll return in a few weeks, then we'll soon be together forever."

"Yes," Amy Jane said. "Forever!"

The next morning before heading back to Savannah, Lawrence sat down and wrote a letter to John Clarke.

Dear Mr. Clarke,

First, I would like to introduce myself. I am Captain Lawrence Wiggins of Savannah, Georgia. I wish that I could properly meet you in person to speak with you about my plans, but since that is impossible, I will do the next best thing - write this letter.

I have fallen in love with your beautiful daughter, Amy Jane. I met her at a summer bar-be-cue, that I was invited to by her grandfather. This was before the war, but I knew that day, I wanted to marry your daughter.

I kept in touch with her after that, by letters from Savannah, before the war. After the war began, I joined the Confederate Army. I was wounded and was taken to the hospital in Atlanta. Who, but lovely Amy Jane, was there to take care of me, of which I am so grateful!

Later, I returned to my company to continue my duties for the Confederate Army. Many times during the heat of battle, Mr. Clarke, the only thing that kept me going was the image of Amy Jane's beautiful face. I knew that I must continue, so that one day when the awful war ended, I could go back to Atlanta and ask Amy Jane to become my wife.

When the war ended, I made my

way to Atlanta with hopes that Amy Jane would still be there. I had asked her, after my stay in the hospital, to wait for me; however, since it seemed that the war would never end, I didn't know if she would wait or not.

Yesterday, I went back to Gable Oaks, hoping Amy Jane had waited for me and she had. So, Mister Clarke, I have asked Amy Jane to become my wife. Would you please allow me the hand of your daughter in marriage? I will so greatly respect your answer whatever it may be.

I am returning to Savannah today to clear up some matters of my father's plantation. He and my mother both died during the war. I will be selling the land.

Before the war, I was studying and working on becoming a lawyer. I hope to set up a law office in Hollow Creek, if there is a need for one.

Please send your reply to my address in Savannah, which I will enclose. I will be waiting there until I receive your blessings or rejection. (I pray for your blessings, for I truly love your daughter.)

Respectfully,
Capt. Lawrence Wiggins

He reread the letter and, after posting it to John, he returned to Savannah to wait for a reply from, he hoped, his future father-in-law.

Chapter Eighteen

The Letter Arrives

Amy Jane was busy making plans to return West for her wedding and to be with her family once again. She received a letter from Lawrence when he returned to Savannah. He wrote that he was getting everything settled. He had sold his father's land and had everything "under control".

He was waiting for a reply from Amy Jane's papa. *As soon as I hear from your papa, with his blessings,* Lawrence wrote, *I will return to my lovely wife-to-be. Then we can be on our way to the great West!*

****

Amy Jane had written to Joy Louisa, telling her all the plans. Joy Louisa was so excited she could hardly keep from telling Ellen and John, but Amy Jane had asked that nothing be said until the letter came from Lawrence.

Joy Louisa began to wonder if this Lawrence, that Amy Jane loved so much, had backed out of writing his letter to John. Several days had passed since Joy Louisa had received her letter from Amy Jane, and still there was not a letter from Lawrence, or either John had not mentioned it.

One day while she was helping Ellen prepare dinner, Joy Louisa mentioned Amy Jane, in hopes, that Ellen would say something about Lawrence. Ellen did not say anything about Lawrence. Joy Louisa felt sure her mama would share exciting news if it had come. *Poor Amy Jane,* Joy Louisa thought, *this southern "gentleman" has gotten "cold feet" and not asked permission from Papa John to marry Amy Jane. She must be heart-broken.*

Joy Louisa continued to prepare the apple pie for dinner, with thoughts of Amy Jane. If Joy Louisa didn't find out soon, she felt that she would surely burst. She must know!

When John and the boys came in from the fields, John had been by the post to pick up the mail. Joy Louisa saw John lay the mail on the table then go over to wash up for dinner.

"Did I get a letter from Amy Jane?" Joy Louisa asked as she took the pie from the oven.

"No," John answered.

"Did you and mama get a letter from Amy Jane?"

"No."

Oh dear, Joy Louisa thought, *that man is not going to write Papa John.*

When the family was seated around the table, Ellen picked up the mail and looked through it.

"John, did ya see this letter?" Ellen asked holding up a letter.

"No, I didn't," John answered. "I looked through the mail to see iffen Joy Louisa had a letter, but I didn't look close to any of the other things. Who's it from?"

"Don't know," Ellen answered. "But it's posted from Savannah, Georgia."

"Savannah? Don't know nobody in Savannah."

"Well, open it," Joy Louisa said impatiently. "It may be important."

"Well, let's pray an' eat first," John replied. "Thet letter can wait, I'm hungry."

"Me, too," Ernest Paul said.

Oh dear, Joy Louisa thought. *How will I ever make it through dinner knowing that letter is sitting there unopened. It has to be from Lawrence. I wonder what Mama and Papa John will say.*

Finally, after what seemed like forever to Joy Louisa, John opened the letter. Everyone sat silently waiting for John to read the letter and tell everyone what it was about. Joy Louisa thought John would never finish reading the letter.

"Well, well," he finally said.

"What is it, dear?" Ellen asked. "Who's the letter from?"

"Captain Lawrence Wiggins," John answered.

"Lawrence? What did he say?" Joy Louisa asked with excitement.

"Do ya know this Lawrence?" John asked.

"No sir," Joy Louisa said shyly, "but Amy Jane has mentioned him in her letters."

"Ok, so ya've known 'bout this?"

"Yes, sir."

"Known 'bout what?" Ellen asked. "What is this all 'bout?"

"Our little Amy Jane has fallen in love," John began. "This letter is from Captain Lawrence Wiggins. He has asked permission fer Amy Jane's hand in marriage."

"Will they be married in Atlanta?" Ellen asked.

"He didn't give any details 'bout a weddin', jest asked permission an' said he would open a law office here in Hollow Creek iffen there was a need fer one. Here, sweetheart," John said as he gave the letter to Ellen, "ya read it."

Ellen gave the letter from Lawrence Wiggins to Joy Louisa. "You read it to all of us, Joy Louisa," Ellen said.

Joy Louisa took the letter from her mother and began to read:

> *Dear Mr. Clarke,*
>
> *First, I would like to introduce myself. I am Captain Lawrence Wiggins of Savannah, Georgia. I wish that I could properly meet you in person to speak with you about my plans, but since that is impossible, I will do the next best thing - write this letter.*
>
> *I have fallen in love with your beautiful daughter, Amy Jane. I met her at a summer bar-be-cue, that I was invited to by her grandfather. This was before the war, but I knew that day, I wanted to marry your daughter.*

"My, my," Ellen said. "My little Amy Jane stole his heart the first time he saw her. Go ahead and finish reading, Joy Louisa."

Joy Louisa began reading:

> *I kept in touch with her after that, by letters from Savannah, before the war. After the war began, I joined the Confederate Army. I was wounded and was taken to the hospital in Atlanta. Who, but lovely Amy Jane, was there to take care of me,*

of which I am so grateful!

"And little Amy Jane was his nurse," Ellen said. The Lord does work in strange ways. Go ahead and read, Joy Louisa, I'll try not to interrupt ya again.

Joy Louisa began to read again.

> *Later, I returned to my company to continue my duties for the Confederate Army. Many times during the heat of battle, Mr. Clarke, the only thing that kept me going was the image of Amy Jane's beautiful face. I knew that I must continue, so that one day when this awful war ended, I could go back to Atlanta and ask Amy Jane to become my wife.*
>
> *When the war ended, I made my way to Atlanta, with hopes that Amy Jane would still be there. I had asked her, after my stay in the hospital, to wait for me; however, since it seemed that the war would never end, I didn't know if she would wait or not.*
>
> *Yesterday, I went back to Gable Oaks, hoping Amy Jane had waited for me and she had.*

"He should have known Amy Jane would wait on him iffen he'd asked her too," Ellen said interrupting again.

"Ellen, sweetheart, would ya let Joy Louisa finish reading the letter?"

"Yes, I'm sorry."

So, Mister Clarke, I have asked Amy Jane to become my wife. Would you please allow me the hand of your daughter in marriage? I will respect your answer whatever it may be.

"Now thet was right nice of him to say thet," Ellen interrupted again. "Oh I'm sorry I keep on a interrupting."

I am returning to Savannah today to clear up some matters of my father's plantation. He and my mother both died during the war. I will be selling the land.

Before the war, I was studying and working on becoming a lawyer. I hope to set up a law office in Hollow Creek, if there is a need for one.

Please send your reply to my address in Savannah, which I will enclose. I will be waiting there until I receive your blessings or rejection. (I pray for your blessings, for I truly love your daughter.)

Respectfully,
Capt. Lawrence Wiggins

As she read it, Joy Louisa wondered if Amy Jane would have the wedding in Atlanta or wait and have it in Hollow Creek. Lawrence didn't say if they would marry before they come to Hollow Creek or not.

"I'm sure Amy Jane has made the right choice," Ellen said. "She would never marry someone who wasn't a Christian."

"Yes, I agree," John said. "I'm sure Catherine would let us know iffen she thought thet it wasn't right."

"Ya need to write Lawrence, soon," Ellen began. "He's pro'bly waitin' fer yo're answer b'fore he makes any more plans."

"Yes, thet's what he wrote. Instead of writin' a letter, thet will take many days, I'll jest go tomorrow an' send him a telegram," John said.

"Thet would be best," Ellen said.

"Could we send one to Amy Jane, too?" Joy Louisa asked.

"I think thet we could," John said smiling. "She's pro'bly worryin' herself to death, wonderin' iffen I'm gonna give her my blessings."

"I'll send Amy Jane a letter, too," Joy Louisa said. "We need to know if she will be married here or in Atlanta."

"I do hope she comes here," Ellen said.

"I hope she does, too," John said. "My little Amy Jane's a gettin' married."

Joy Louisa and Ellen made plans and talked about the wedding that they hoped to be a part of. Joy Louisa was so excited she could hardly contain herself. Later, she sat down and wrote a letter to Amy Jane.

The next morning, John sent off two telegrams, one to Lawrence and one to Amy Jane.

The one sent to Lawrence read:

To Captain Wiggins - stop -
My Blessings are with you - stop -

You have my permission for the hand
of Amy Jane - stop -
Your future papa - in - law -stop -
John Clarke - stop -

The one sent to Amy Jane read:

To my lovely daughter - stop -
You and Captain Wiggins have
my blessings - stop -
Come home for wedding - stop -
Please - stop -
Love you - stop -
Mama and Papa - stop -

When Amy Jane received the telegram she cried. She was happy her father had given her his blessings. She longed to go home and she hoped Lawrence would come soon.

Lawrence was pleased when he received his telegram from John. It had been two weeks since the letter had been sent to Amy Jane's father and because he was unaware the letter had been delayed, Lawrence had begun to worry. But now he held his long awaited answer. Tomorrow, he would go to Atlanta!

Early the following morning Lawrence headed for Atlanta. He did not let Amy Jane know he was coming for two reasons. The first was that he did not know exactly when he would be hearing from John, and the second reason was that he wanted to surprise Amy Jane. Lawrence loved seeing the excitement on Amy Jane's face when he arrived at Gable Oaks. He thought now as he was headed to Atlanta, of the look on her face the day he rode to Gable Oaks after he had been away so long.

Chapter Nineteen

A Yankee Soldier Visits

After Amy Jane read and reread the telegram from her papa, she sat down and wrote a long letter to him.

Dear Papa,

Thank you so much for giving your blessings to me and Lawrence. You'll never have any reason to regret it. Lawrence is a wonderful Christian man, but then you would know that I would never marry anyone who wasn't a Christian. You've always taught me that principle, for which I am very grateful.

I haven't heard from Lawrence in a week now. I guess he's waiting to hear from you. As soon as he comes back to Atlanta, we will then start making our plans to travel West.

Aunt Catherine, Velvet, Agnes and her little son are all planning on making the trip with us. I had to convince Aunt Catherine that it would be all right with mama for my southern family to come West. Aunt Catherine was afraid that since she was Mama Rachel's sister, that Mama Ellen would not want them. Now ain't that just silly? But if Mama wants to write Aunt Catherine and let her know they are welcome, that would be good.

Aunt Catherine and Velvet have really been a big help to me on making plans for the wedding. Oh, Papa, Grandmother Ellis still had Mama Rachel's wedding dress. If it's all right with you, I want to wear that dress. It is so lovely! Grandmother showed it to me when I first came to Atlanta. When I put the dress on Grandmother cried. She said I looked just like "her Rachel".

I have a bit of sad news to tell you since I've mentioned Grandmother Ellis. She died during the war. Age crept up on her and slowed her way down; but the stress of the war put the finishing touch of death on her.

Aunt Catherine, Velvet, and I were around her bedside, and, as Aunt Catherine read from the Bible, a Yankee soldier walked into the bed room. This totally shocked us ladies, but Grandmother Ellis acted as if she were not afraid at all. She leaned up and with a weak voice asked the soldier if she could help him. He wanted to know where the silver and gold were hidden.

Grandmother told him that

she had no treasures hid on this earth. She told him all of her treasures were laid up in a different place. He demanded to know where. He told her if she did not tell him, he would search the entire house until he found them. Grandmother told him her treasures were laid up in heaven, and then she fell back on her pillow.

After her death, grandfather was never the same again. He died a short time later. Gable Oaks would never be the same again without these two precious people. They were truly great people. But let me go on with the rest of what I was writing.

Tell Mama and Joy Louisa that I'll need all the help I can get from them when I get home. Let Uncle Edward know that he'll be performing the ceremony.

Oh, Papa, I'm so excited! Not only about my marriage to Lawrence, but also, I will soon be coming home! Won't it be just wonderful? I'll send you a telegram as soon as I find out the train schedule and the time we will be arriving. It doesn't seem possible that when I left Hollow Creek there wasn't a train coming through there, and now there's a station right in town. I guess I won't even know Hollow Creek when I arrive, will I?

Tell my little brothers and sister

that I will soon be home. I just hope they will still know me. It seems like it has been forever since I've been home. Not too much longer now!

I'm just rattling on and on. I need to get busy, so I'll say good-bye for now. I love you, Papa! Thanks for your blessings on my marriage. I'll live up to your teachings! Promise!

With Much Love
your daughter,
Amy Jane

****

Amy Jane was packing some of her things she would be taking West with her when she heard the sound of a horse. She ran to the door hoping Lawrence had arrived. When she walked out on the porch, she froze with fright. There sitting on a big black and beautiful horse was a Yankee soldier. Amy Jane recognized the soldier as the same one who had come to Gable Oaks the day Grandmother Ellis died.

It seemed time stood still for Amy Jane. She wanted to run, but her feet would not move. It seemed they were glued to the porch. She then felt as if she would faint.

The Yankee soldier slid from his horse and walked slowly toward Amy Jane. He knew that he should not have come back, but he had to apologize to this family. The memories of that day he walked in and the old lady died had haunted him throughout the war.

"Aunt Catherine! Aunt Catherine! Aunt Catherine!" Amy Jane screamed in terror.

Catherine ran to the door just as the soldier stepped on the porch. When he stepped onto the porch Amy Jane fainted.

"Velvet, Agnes!" Catherine called. "Come quick!"

"I'm sorry, ma'am," the soldier began. "I didn't mean to frighten the lady."

"That's all right," Catherine said. She did not recognize the young soldier.

Velvet rushed to Amy Jane. Agnes walked out onto the porch to talk with the soldier. *He is quite handsome,* Agnes thought.

"How may we help you, sir?" Agnes asked.

The soldier watched as Velvet and Catherine helped Amy Jane inside the house. Then he looked at Agnes.

"I have come to make an apology to the family that lived here during the war," the soldier said.

"My grandmother and grandfather owned this plantation during the war," Agnes began. "They are both dead now."

"Yes, I know," the soldier said sadly.

"I don't understand," Agnes said. "How did you know they were dead? You're a Yankee soldier, why should you care about who lived here and if they were dead or not?"

"Were you here when your grandmother died?" the soldier asked.

"Well, no, I wasn't, but I really don't feel that it is any of your business," Agnes said. "You and all *the rest* of the Yankees got what you wanted, so what does it matter to you now?"

"I would like to speak to the other three ladies if I may," he said. "That is if they will allow me to."

"I don't know if they will talk with you or not," Agnes replied.

"Yes, I know and I understand if they refuse, but I really do need to talk with them."

While Agnes talked with the soldier, Amy Jane told Catherine and Velvet about what had just happened.

"Aunt Catherine, do you know who that man is?" Amy Jane asked in alarm.

"No. I guess I don't," Catherine replied.

"He is the Yankee soldier who walked in the house the day Grandmother died."

"Are you sure?" Catherine asked.

"Oh, yes ma'am, I'm sure! He asked Grandmother where she kept her treasures and she told him that her treasures were in heaven. She then fell back on her pillows and died. Don't you remember?"

"Yes, I remember that, but are you sure he is *that* soldier?"

"Yes, ma'am. I could never forget him," Amy Jane said. "So many nights after the death of Grandmother, I dreamed of that soldier coming into Grandmother's room."

"Ok," Catherine said. "I'll go out and ask him what he wants."

"I'll go with you," Amy Jane said. "I feel better now."

"And I'll go, too," Velvet said.

The three ladies walked out onto the porch and as they stepped outside the soldier walked over to them.

"I'm so sorry that I frightened you, miss," he said.

"What *are* you doing here?" Catherine asked.

"Well, ma'am, I want to apologize to the three ladies who lived here during the war."

"That will be the three here," Catherine said motioning her hand to herself, Velvet and Amy Jane.

"Ladies, first I would like to introduce myself. My name is Bernie Woodson and I'm from Ohio. When the war first began in this area I came to this house to steal from you."

The soldier paused, wiped his brow with the back of his hand, then he continued. "When I walked upstairs, you three ladies were sitting with an elderly lady."

"Yes," Catherine said. "That was my mother."

"I asked where I could find the valuables of this house," the soldier continued. "The little old lady said that her treasures were laid up in heaven, then she fell back on her pillows and I assumed she went to her treasures."

"Yes," Catherine answered. "She had a weak heart and when she saw you, a Yankee soldier, standing in her door asking for her valuables, it was more than she could handle."

"I want to say that I am so sorry that happened," the soldier said sadly. "When I saw her fall back I felt she was gone. I stood there several minutes, wanting to help, but I knew that you would not let me."

"You're probably right," Velvet put in.

"When I saw you three ladies gathered around the bedside, I wasn't really seeing you. I was seeing my three sisters gathered around my mother's bedside."

The soldier paused and wiped away a tear. "You see my mother also had a weak heart. When I told her that I was joining up with the Union Army, she could not bear the thought of her only son going to war. She died the same way your mother died," the soldier said, looking at Catherine.

"I'm sorry," Catherine said with compassion.

"Later," the soldier continued, "when Sherman came through Atlanta I was among that group of soldiers. In fact, I was a Sergeant over a company of men. I was given orders to go through every house, clean out all the goods and burn the houses."

He paused, took a deep breath and continued, "When I realized that I was in this house, I again saw my three sisters gathered around my mother's bedside. I knew I had caused grief once to this plantation and I was not going to do it again. The men did set fire to one of the cabins and went through the house before I realized where I was. They asked me about burning the house and I would not let them. They asked me if I was becoming a softy, but I was determined not to bring anymore sorrow to this family."

"We appreciate that very much," Catherine said.

"Constantly, during the war, that scene came before me, then it would change to my own mother and sisters. I vowed to God, if the war ever ended and I was alive, I would come and apologize to you. I prayed for your safety every night."

The soldier looked from Catherine to Velvet then to Amy Jane. "Will you ladies, please forgive me? I am sorry. I know I can't bring your loved one back, but I do hope you can forgive me for what I did."

"Yes, sir," Catherine said. "You are forgiven. We thank you for not letting your men burn our house down."

"And miss," the soldier began, turning to Amy Jane. "I am sorry that I gave you such a scare earlier."

"That's ok," Amy Jane said. "I recognized you and it just upset me."

"Yes ma'am. I can understand why."

Agnes walked over to the group and looked at the soldier. "We're about to have dinner, would you honor us by accepting my invitation?"

The soldier heard the gasp of Velvet and Amy Jane and was about to refuse when Catherine agreed.

"That would be fine, sir," Catherine was saying. "The war is now over and we should have peace with all men."

Chapter Twenty

Agnes & Bernie Woodson

Amy Jane sat upright in her bed, her heart racing within her body. Then she realized it was only a dream. She saw the Yankee soldier standing in the doorway of Grandmother Ellis' room. It seemed so real, why had this come back to her again?

Then she remembered the evening before when she ran to the front door at the sound of horse's hooves. She thought Lawrence was returning from Savannah. When she went out on the front porch she saw the Yankee soldier. The entire scene came to her once again.

Agnes had been foolish enough to invite the Yankee soldier to stay for dinner and he accepted. Aunt Catherine agreed with Agnes. Amy Jane had never wanted dinner to pass so fast in her life, yet it seemed time stood still.

Amy Jane thought how Agnes had flirted with the Yankee soldier. He seemed to enjoy the attention he received from Agnes. She asked him to join her in the parlor for coffee and pie after dinner. Little Samuel seemed to enjoy the soldier's attention.

It would be good if Agnes could marry again and find a good man to be a papa to little Samuel. Surely not a Yankee! Agnes had made a mistake when she married Tom Morgan. Amy Jane prayed that Agnes wouldn't fall for this Yankee soldier.

As Amy Jane lay listening to the crickets sing through her opened window, she thought of her two cousins. Agnes was totally different from her sister, Velvet. Agnes always wanted to be seen and heard. She was always flirting, even since she had become a widow. She had long put off her black mourning attire.

The Yankee soldier seemed really to like little Samuel. He *was* a darling little boy and needed a father figure. Someone who would help him to learn how to farm the land when he was older. But not a Yankee!

Amy Jane turned over trying to forget the Yankee soldier, but it seemed his face would not go away. She lay there a few more minutes listening to the crickets and frogs. Finally, she dozed off to sleep.

The next evening, just before dinner, the Yankee soldier returned to Gable Oaks. He brought a rose for each of the ladies and a piece of candy for Samuel. Of course, Agnes asked the soldier to stay for dinner. Afterwards, the two of them walked out in the rose garden.

"Mama, I don't like what I see," Velvet said as she, Catherine and Amy Jane sat in the parlor. "Agnes don't even know that man. He's a Yankee!"

"Now, Velvet, we can't judge the man just because he is a Yankee," Catherine said. "I, too, feel he is trying to win Agnes' heart. I do need to speak with her about this."

"She enjoys the attention he's giving her," Velvet said.

"Yes, but she is still young and needs someone to love her," Catherine was saying. "I just hope she doesn't do the same thing that she did with Tom."

"Well, I wouldn't be surprised," Velvet said. "Especially, if you tell her she can't have him as a caller."

"She is now a woman with a child on her own Velvet," Catherine said. " There's not a whole lot I can do."

"I understand that," Velvet replied, "but you can stop that Yankee from coming to our house."

"Yes, I could, but if he wins her heart, then she will run off with him like she did Tom. Not only will she go, but she will take Samuel from us."

"That's very true," Velvet said sadly. "I sure would hate for Agnes to take little Samuel off somewhere, especially to Yankee land."

"Velvet, we must love the Yankees. I would hate for Agnes to take Samuel from us, too," Catherine began, "but we're going to have to realize that Samuel is Agnes' child. She will not be here with us forever."

"I know," Velvet said, "but to Yankee territory, that would be horrible!"

****

Later that evening, Amy Jane was hemming a dress for Velvet. There was a sound of a horse's hooves coming up the drive. At first, Amy Jane thought perhaps Bernie Woodson was leaving, but instead of the sound going away, it was coming closer.

Is that Lawrence? Amy Jane thought to herself. As the sound drew closer, Amy Jane ran to the window. She pulled back the curtains just as the horse and rider pulled to halt. Lawrence looked up and saw Amy Jane as she disappeared behind the curtains.

Smiling to himself, Lawrence jumped off the horse. Before he had the time to tie the horse to the post, Amy Jane was running down the steps.

"My beautiful Amy Jane," Lawrence said pulling her into his arms. "You must have slid down the rail instead of coming down the stairs."

"Oh, Lawrence," Amy Jane laughed. "I didn't think you would ever get back. It seems like ages since I've seen you."

"I'm here now sweetheart to stay. I have a room at the Boarding House in town until we leave for the West."

"Now we can begin to make our plans to head West," Amy Jane said.

"We sure can," Lawrence answered. "By the way, who's riding that nice looking horse?"

"A Yankee soldier."

"A What?!?"

"A Yankee soldier," Amy Jane replied.

"What is a Yankee soldier doing here at Gable Oaks," Lawrence asked.

"Well, it's a long story. You remember me telling you about the Yankee soldier that came in the house the day Grandmother Ellis died?"

"Yes."

"Well, he came back to apologize."

"To apologize for what?" Lawrence asked.

"He thought Grandmother died when she saw him, which she really did. Her heart was bad and when he came in demanding all the valuables, she fell back on her pillow - dead."

Amy Jane paused a moment then continued, "He said when he saw me, Velvet and Aunt Catherine gathered around Grandmother's bed, the scene he *really* saw was back in Ohio. When he told his mother he was joining the Union Army, she couldn't bear the thought of losing her only son. Her heart was bad, too, and she died the same way Grandmother died."

"How long has he been here?" Lawrence asked.

"Today - only a few hours."

"Today? You mean he's been here more than just today?" Lawrence asked.

"Yes. He came for the first time, yesterday."

"Then why is he back here again today?" Lawrence asked in complete surprise.

"I think he has fallen for Agnes."

"Surely Agnes wouldn't fall for a Yankee!"

"That's what I said, but it looks as if it has happened," Amy Jane said.

Lawrence followed Amy Jane's gaze and saw Agnes walking up the lane with the Yankee soldier. She was looking up at him all starry eyed.

"I can't believe it," Lawrence said.

"I know, but she has always been that way - easy to *fall in love*, Velvet told me. She ran off and married Tom Morgan just before the war started. Aunt Catherine forbade Agnes to marry Tom, so one night when everyone was asleep, she left Aunt Catherine a note. The note stated that Tom was coming to take Agnes to Savannah. They were getting married before Tom had to go off to war."

Agnes and Bernie noticed that Amy Jane and Lawrence had glanced toward them.

"Well, well, who's the fellow there with your cousin?" Bernie asked.

"That's Captain Lawrence Wiggins, he and Amy Jane are getting married soon," Agnes said.

"He's getting a mighty pretty lady for his wife," Bernie said.

"Now, you're making me jealous," Agnes said, pouting.

"Now, Agnes, dear, I'm sorry. You are beautiful. Any man in his right mind would want to marry you."

"Oh Bernie," Agnes said laying her hand on Bernie's arm. *Then why don't you ask me to marry you,* Agnes thought.

"You know I would love to take a beautiful lady like you back to Ohio as my wife," Bernie said.

"Really?"

"Yes, but I'm sure your mother would not approve of her lovely - southern belle - daughter marrying a Yankee soldier."

"No, she probably wouldn't approve, but I'm a woman now. I've been a widow long enough. I can make my own decisions."

"But you don't even know me, Agnes," Bernie said.

"Well, anybody who would return to a house to apologize for something he *really* didn't do, can't be too bad of a man."

"I did cause your Grandmother's death."

"No, Bernie, you didn't cause Grandmother to die. She had a bad heart for many years. She would have died sooner or later."

"I guess you're right," Bernie said. "I know we just met yesterday, but I'm heading back to Ohio in two days and I'd like to take you back with me as my wife. Could you be ready to leave in two days?"

"I probably could."

"Good. I'll go tomorrow and purchase a train ticket for me and you," Bernie said.

"You will allow Samuel to go, won't you?" Agnes asked with concern.

"Certainly, " Bernie answered. "I know you would never leave your son. I will take him as if he were my very own. I may be a Yankee, but I'm a Christian Yankee."

The couple walked back to the house and into the parlor where the other family members were sitting and talking. Agnes introduced Bernie to Lawrence, then the two were seated. Lawrence felt uncomfortable sitting in the same room with the "enemy". A few minutes later, Lawrence asked Amy Jane if she would like to take a walk through the flower garden. Soon after Amy Jane and Lawrence left the room, Velvet decided to go to her room.

Bernie thought this would be a good opportunity to talk with Catherine about the plans of taking Agnes and Samuel to Ohio. Bernie was afraid that Catherine was going to leave the room several times, but each time he thought Catherine was about to leave, Agnes would say something to her mother.

After a moment of silence, Bernie said, "Mrs. Catherine, I have something very important to talk with you about."

"Yes?"

"I would like to take your daughter as my wife... Please wait a minute," Bernie said when Catherine was about to interrupt. "Please let me finish, then you can tell us how you feel."

"Very well," Catherine said with a sigh.

"I know that we just met yesterday and I know a real southern mother does not want her daughter to marry a Yankee soldier. I may be a Yankee soldier, but like I told Agnes, I am a Christian Yankee. I am leaving for Ohio in two days and I would like to take Agnes and Samuel with me."

Catherine sighed and shook her head sadly, then looking at her daughter, Catherine began, "Agnes, you have been taught the proper way to enter into a marriage. You disobeyed me the first time you were married. Now from that marriage you have a son to raise from the husband who was killed in a cruel war.

I know you are now a woman on your own and there's not much I can do about any decision that you make. I am, however, totally against this marriage. You do not know one another and your backgrounds are very different. Agnes, this truly breaks my heart. I don't know where I went wrong in your up-bringing.

Catherine paused, wiping away her tears, then continued, "Again, as with your first marriage, you do not have my blessings. You must think this over - you are taking your small son into a totally different environment than he has been in all of his life. I pray you will make the right decision."

Catherine left the room.

"Everything your mother has said is so true, Agnes, dear, maybe we should…"

"No, Bernie, don't say that," Agnes began. "We are both Christians and Samuel needs a good father. I know we can make it."

"Yes, dear. I'm sure we can."

Chapter Twenty-one

Sad Farewells

Two days later Bernie arrived at Gable Oaks with the train tickets for himself, Agnes and little Samuel. Catherine felt heart broken once again by the actions of her daughter. It seemed nothing Catherine could say to Agnes would change her mind. She was determined to marry the Yankee soldier.

Catherine wondered where she had gone wrong in rearing Agnes. She just could not understand why Agnes would want to do such an awful thing. Silently, Amy Jane watched in the distance as Catherine said her tearful good-byes.

"Please, Agnes, don't go," Catherine begged. "This can't be the right thing. You don't know Bernie nor his family."

"Oh, mother, you worry too much," Agnes said without any feeling.

Catherine sat on the couch and wept. Agnes went upstairs to bring down some of her belongings.

"Agnes," Velvet said softly as she entered Agnes' bedroom.

"Now don't you start on me, too," Agnes said. "I'm tired of living the way we've had to live since the war. Look at my clothes. They are nothing compared to what I had before the war. The Yankees have all the money, now, so why not join them."

"Oh, Agnes," was all Velvet could say. Then with tears streaming down her cheeks, Velvet walked over to Agnes. "I love you, Agnes. Please take care of yourself and little Samuel. If you ever need to come home, you know you will always be welcome. You *will* come back to visit with us, won't you, Agnes?"

"Yes, Velvet. I'll come back with all the finest clothes money can buy," Agnes said with a smile. "I won't have to wear these dresses any longer. Bernie said he would buy me and Samuel anything we wanted."

"It's not all in material things, Agnes," Velvet said. "All these things will fade away. We must put our lives in God's hand."

"You heard Bernie say he was a Christian, Velvet," Agnes said impatiently. "You don't have to be like Mother and worry so much. He'll take me to church, I'm sure."

"Just be careful, Agnes. I love you, big sister," Velvet said through tears.

"I love you, too, little sister," Agnes said.

Before she turned away, Velvet was sure she saw tears in Agnes' eyes. Velvet turned and walked out of the room and back downstairs to where her mother was sitting in the parlor.

As Velvet entered the parlor, she noticed her mother talking with Bernie. Amy Jane was sitting on the floor playing with Samuel, so Velvet joined them.

"Mrs. Catherine," Bernie was saying, "I know this is not the proper way to do this and I have talked with Agnes concerning what we are about to do. She is set to go on with me now."

"Yes, she has always been a very stubborn child," Catherine said shaking her head. "You must learn to live with that, Bernie."

"Yes, ma'am," Bernie answered.

"I want to make it understood to you and Agnes that I do *not* approve of this courtship and especially this marriage. I do not approve of the two of you traveling together, not married, to Ohio. That is not the proper, nor Christian, thing to do."

"Yes, ma'am," Bernie answered. "Mrs. Catherine, I don't want to sound rude, but I know that I am Yankee by birth, but I *am* also a Christian by choice. I *do* know what is proper and what is not. I also know it is not proper for the two of us to travel as unmarried companions; therefore, I have already made the arrangements for Agnes and me to be married before the train leaves this evening."

"I see," Catherine replied.

"I would like very much for you and the rest of the family to join us today at two o'clock for the ceremony. It will not be anything fancy, but it will be in the church. Pastor Collins will perform the ceremony. Agnes and I sat down and talked with him last evening."

"If you don't mind me asking, how does Pastor Collins feel about this?" Catherine asked.

"He also thinks it is not a good idea for Agnes to marry a Yankee, and I can understand why you Southern people would feel that way. The war is over now, and we must continue our lives. I know it's not natural to fall in love at first sight, but I have."

Bernie sat quiet for a moment then continued, "To be perfectly honest with you, Mrs. Catherine, Agnes reminds me a lot of my own mother. I promise you that I will take care of and provide for Agnes and Samuel."

"I trust that you will," Catherine answered.

****

"Miz Catherine," Sadie began, "I knows thet ya don' think Agnes is doin' the right thing, but I wunt to fix up a dinnah fo' her an' de fellow after de weddin', dat is if ya' don' mind. I thinks it ain't fittin' to habe one of de Hester girls to be married an' not habe a dinnah."

"Well, Sadie, I don't know," Catherine said. "I don't want them to think that I approve of this marriage, but then again they will need something to eat before they leave for Ohio."

"Yas'm, I thought de same thing. I starts fix'n' somethin' now. Does yo' mind if I'se bake de las' cake?"

"No, Sadie, do whatever you wish to do," Catherine replied.

"Oh, thank ya', Miz Catherine. You knows how I loves thet chile an' de little Samuel. I'se sho' nuff gwine miss dem."

"Yes, Sadie, we will all surely miss them," Catherine said. "I just pray they will be a happy family together."

"Yas'm I prays thet too. Dem two daughters ob yorn' be two precious chur'n," Sadie said.

"They are totally different, but they are precious," Catherine answered.

"I needs to starts wiff de dinnah, so's it be ready when eber body gets back heah."

Sadie hurried for the kitchen to begin preparing the wedding meal. She knew it wasn't *really* 'fittin' to have the fancy meal, since Catherine didn't approve, but she loved Agnes and wanted to do something special for her. She would soon be leaving Gable Oaks and Sadie didn't know when or if ever she would see the 'chile' again.

Sadie called Cozetta into the kitchen, "Cozetta, I needs fo' ya to helps me wiff dis dinnah."

"Whut you fixin' a big dinnah fo'?" Cozetta asked.

"Don' ya ax no questions, you jist do as yo' mama tells you to do. We's gwine fix up a good dinnah fer Miz Agnes an' de new husband. I'se gwine bake a purtty cake fer dem. So I needs fer you to starts wiff de washin' of de p'tatoes."

"Yas'm," Cozetta answered. "Whut else is you gwine ta fix?"

I don' know. I'se figure out somethin'. I needs to find Otis an' Carl. Dey needs to catch me some ob dem chick'ns."

Sadie rushed around the kitchen trying to arrange everything for the dinner. She had Otis and Carl out catching, cleaning and dressing the chickens. Cozetta was busy preparing vegetables and Sadie was baking a cake. She wanted to have everything completed and ready when the family returned from the wedding.

Just before two o'clock everyone at Gable Oaks was busy preparing to go to the church for Agnes' wedding. Catherine cried as she dressed for, what should have been, a happy occasion. She hoped and prayed that Agnes would be happy. *She had been a widow a long time and she really needed someone to care for her,* Catherine thought to herself.

The group made their way to the church. Bernie awaited their arrival. Catherine thought, *now Bernie does looks very attractive and he appears to be a good Christian as well.*

Agnes smiled when she saw Bernie at the front door of the church. Amy Jane prayed that Agnes had made the right choice. The feelings that love bring are unsurpassed; however, Amy Jane thought this seemed too soon for Agnes and Bernie.

The couple made their way to the front of the church with Pastor Collins, while the rest of the family sat on the front pew. Pastor Collins read from the Bible, had the couple to exchange vows, then he pronounced the two husband and wife.

"They do make a pretty couple, don't they?" Velvet whispered to Amy Jane.

"Yes, I was thinking the same thing," Amy Jane answered.

When the pastor completed the ceremony, Catherine hugged both the bride and groom. "I love you, Agnes," Catherine said through tears. Then turning to Bernie she said, "Please take care of my daughter and grandson, and welcome into our family."

"Thank you, Mother Catherine," Bernie said smiling. "And I will take care of your daughter and grandson. I promise."

"What time does the train leave?" Catherine asked.

"It doesn't leave until six o'clock this evening." Bernie answered. "I have already taken the trunks to the station."

"Sadie has a wedding dinner prepared for us at Gable Oaks," Catherine said. "She asked me if she could create a special dinner. So if we're all finished here, we can head back to Gable Oaks for a wedding dinner."

"Thank you, Mother," Agnes said, giving her mother a hug. "Thank you so much."

Sadie placed the best china, linens and silver on the table. Cozetta had cut some roses from the rose garden and made a beautiful center piece for the table.

"Oh, Sadie," Agnes said through tears as she saw the lovely table set with the finest things of Gable Oaks. "This looks lovely. Thank you so much for everything."

"Honey chile," Sadie began with tears streaming down her cheeks. "Ya's been dear to my heart fo' many years. I'se wants the best fo' you an' yo' chile. Dis is all dat I could do fo' you. So I ax Miz Catherine to lets me make ya a good dinnah fo' you left Gable Oaks."

"Thank you so much," Agnes said giving the old Negro maid a hug.

****

The family stood and watched as Agnes, Bernie and Samuel took their places in the carriage. Otis carried them to the train station. It was a sad farewell. Catherine stood waving until the carriage continued out of sight.

"Lord, be with the new family," Catherine prayed as she walked back into the house.

The family gathered in the parlor. The house seemed empty without little Samuel running around. Velvet felt a wave of sadness when she thought of Agnes and Samuel.

After they were seated, Catherine asked, "Well, Amy Jane and Lawrence when do you plan to head West?"

"I have everything taken care of in Savannah," Lawrence began. "I need to settle some business here in Atlanta and check on when we can obtain a train ticket."

"You and Velvet are still going with us, aren't you, Aunt Catherine?" Amy Jane asked.

"Oh, Mama, you said we could go, and I really would love to go," Velvet exclaimed.

"Are you sure your mother won't mind us coming, Amy Jane?" Catherine asked with concern.

"Oh, no!" Amy Jane exclaimed. "She would love to have you come and stay just as long as you want to stay."

"We'll only go for the wedding," Catherine said. "We would not want to intrude on the family."

"Please, Aunt Catherine, don't even think of something like that," Amy Jane said. "Mama is such a wonderful person. She will welcome you with open arms, and I know Papa would enjoy having you to visit with the family."

"If you would write them ahead of time," Catherine said. "I don't want to arrive and them not know we are coming."

" I have already written them to let them know you all will make the trip; however, I will send them a telegram tomorrow," Amy Jane answered. "Then we can be on our way in a few weeks, or whenever Lawrence can get us a ticket. The sooner the better!"

BOOKS BY BRENDA DUKE-BARBER

JOY IN WINTER
COME SPRING
A SUMMER OF LOVE

To order additional copies of the above books, complete the information below:

Ship to: (Please print)

Name____

Address______________________________________

City, State, Zip_______________________________

______copies of ***Joy In Winter*** @ $7.99 ea. $______

______copies of ***Come Spring*** @ $7.99 ea. $______

______copies of ***A Summer of Love*** @ $7.99 ea. $______

Postage and handling @ 15% per book $______

Total amount enclosed $______

Make checks payable to: ***Brenda Duke-Barber***

Send to: P. O. Box 641
Gainesville, GA 30503